COLORADO TWILIGHT

MARK W. BALDWIN

iUniverse, Inc.
Bloomington

Colorado Twilight

iUniverse books may be ordered through booksellers or by contacting:

iUniverse
1663 Liberty Drive
Bloomington, IN 47403
www.iuniverse.com
1-800-Authors (1-800-288-4677)

ISBN: 978-1-4502-6968-1 (sc)
ISBN: 978-1-4502-6967-4 (ebk)

Printed in the United States of America

iUniverse rev. date: 11/29/2010

CHAPTER 1
SURVIVAL

The lone figure huddled against the cold breeze of the early morning Colorado twilight. A light dusting of frost covered the scraggly grass, bushes and trees around him.

Wayne Parnell waited patiently. He had learned patience when he was a young boy living with his family in a tent. Patience got you a fish for dinner, or other prizes. Patience tempered the soul and kept you alive in difficult times. Conserve energy today and you will be able to hunt tomorrow, if there were anything left *to* hunt.

He and his family had lived in a nine by twelve-foot tent for almost a year and a half. His step father had been a liar, a cheat, a thief, and would not work a job to save his life. Most of the time they survived by poaching whatever they could find. Rabbits, squirrels, fish and deer, if they could get it, it was dinner. The weirdest thing he remembered about living in the tent was that before they cooked red meat in their blue tent, it looked green. He smiled as he remembered the book "Green Eggs and Ham."

In his early 50's, he was lean and strong. His wizened face reflected intelligence, determination, resolve, and etched lines of sadness. All that he knew from his past was now only a memory. The nukes and conventional bombs made sure of that. There were no retirements, no movie theaters, no Diners, and no car dealers. The society that he knew and sometimes loathed was nothing but charred rubble, or full of radiation. He did not know if the rest of his family in Oregon were alive or not. He promised himself that someday, somehow, he would make it back there to find out.

Shifting quietly from one foot to another, he reflected on the circumstances that led him to this place. He thought of when he was a teenager he and his brothers played in the forests, hiding amongst the trees, tracking each other. Little did they know that the meager skills they developed would help keep them alive decades later. Many people throughout the years scoffed at him for his views about how awful the future was going to be. For years, he stored supplies, ammunition, food, and the like. The bunker he drew up several years earlier became a reality only a few years before the bombs. This was the reality he saw coming. This was what he prepared his body and mind for. Now they were probably dead, and he was not.

The bow in his hand and the arrows in the quiver were for the quiet hunt. Hungry men that survived off the land might still be around. For *those*, he kept his weapons prepared. Sure a gun called attention to you, but for those that had no guns, the sound scared them off. His belief in "one shot, one kill" also persuaded would be killers and thieves. Of the several people he had to kill, he buried with respect, but they went into the ground with nothing. He kept everything of use. He was no thief and would not take from others, unless they preyed on others and/or had no scruples. The law of the land was now kill or be killed.

The whole mess started with the open Mexican border, where most of them freely crossed into the bordering state. They kept coming. America's southern border was almost wide open to the multitudes of desperate people, the cutthroats, and the religious fanatics. Certain men and women of the hoards carried the key ingredients, but if lost, could be replaced, although not easily. All over the country they spread, hoarding their precious cargo. Nearly all of the EMP (Electro Magnetic Pulse) units were completed. So were the dirty bombs. They had been dedicated to their cause and had patience. More than a thousand of both were assembled all over the country.

The time was preset, and all but a few accomplished their mission. After that, the missiles came and did the worst damage. Almost all of the assemblers died so they could go to their version of heaven.

Many of the hardened bunkers survived as had their electronics. Almost all of the military bases, airports and major cities are now gone. Retaliatory strikes from the US and their allies destroyed the several countries that made the attack. All countries had been affected from the fallout. The darkened skies destroyed almost as much as the bombs and radiation. All told more than five billion died, and it was all started in the name of religion.

After the bombs had stopped falling, things were exceedingly bad. Only a few EMP shielded radios transmitted the horror and devastation across the once mighty United States. Stores became bare within hours. Radiation killed more than the initial blasts, though in many cases, it took a long, miserable time to do it. The local wildlife had been devastated when hungry people moved into the hills. Only the hardiest animals that were best suited for mountain life were able to keep away from the painful bite of lead. Within a few weeks, most people started running out of food. Several weeks later the stench of rotting bodies was overwhelming.

If the radiation did not get them, gangs, looters, or crazy people did. They eventually ended up killing each other for food and clean water.

City dwellers died by the millions.

Those that could form small co-ops in the farmlands survived longer, but the hungry multitudes kept coming. Death by bullet was better than by hunger. A few months later 96% of the population were dead. There were still bands of rovers that kept away from the radiation zones. Most of them had planned for the future, but not for the devastation to come. Some came to eating their dead. Moving from area to area, scavenging what they could, they lived with sickness and death.

The dozens and dozens of boxes that the man put aside were a conglomeration of everything he could think of for survival. There was more than just survival gear, for people needed things to do, books to read, games to play, survival strategies to figure out. He had the foresight to build his bunker well. Buried back in the hills near the Rocky Mountains, it had a deep well with a hand pump, a bathroom with a solar heated shower, a kitchen with a dining table, a library, lots of 12-volt batteries, a solar battery charger, an armory, food storage, and two escape tunnels. It also had small light tubes, that ran from just above ground level to inside the bunker. They could be covered from the inside at night, so the feeble light inside could not be seen outside.

There was a smaller, fake, bunker that was less well hidden. If someone were to get into it, he would only find a small cot and empty shelves. They would not think to search further, for the false wall leading into the main building.

The skills and knowledge that he lacked, he had researched and printed out. There were pages and pages of natural foods, berries, tubers, flowers and plants. He printed out ways to trap animals and ways to tan hides. This would become his bible. He had also stocked up on farming, survival, medical, and natural foods and medicinal plant books.

He had felt so lucky when the chaos started. His wife had prepared several more boxes of canned foods, and other supplies, and they had been in the mountains stocking up their shelter. His older brother Dane had wanted to come along since he had not been out there for several months. The mountains protected them from the blasts and EMP. He had bought parts for his vehicle to protect it only a few years before. After arming themselves and grabbing their NBC gear, they rushed home to grab what they could. They had been dismayed at the fallout and the chaos around them and on the highways.

Cars were stalled all over the roads. He had almost had to run a few men over to keep from getting stopped by them. A few frantic people waved guns at him as he sped by. When they got to the house, Dane stayed with the car with his NBC gear on, complete with a gas mask. He stood guard with an old British .303. It was loaded and had the safety off.

The plan was to be loaded and back on the road in fifteen minutes. The car had been stuffed from hastily shoving in loads of food, clothes and bedding. A few mementos were quickly added just before heading out. Although he did not think it would help, he had locked the house up just in case they could come back sometime soon. At the time, he did not know how serious the attack was.

On the way back, someone took a shot at them when they did not stop to help. The shelter was only designed for a maximum of six people. They would have been swamped by the mob if they stopped. They had all agreed in advance that stopping for anyone could mean death to one or all of them.

Once they were safely back at the shelter and unloaded, they quickly covered the car with a camouflage tarp. Once they shut the shelter door, they did not come back out for several months.

In retrospect, they had all been remarkably lucky.

He did not curse his luck, his life or his circumstances. This is what life was now, and he was doing his best to protect his family. Even though they had it good, he knew that at some point, they would need to find others.

He thought of the years of canning vegetables from the garden, of the chickens he and his wife raised, slaughtered and canned. He had stored seeds and planted different varieties of fruit-bearing trees near the shelter. He had planted them far enough apart that it did not draw undue attention.

Leaning against an Aspen tree in his winter camouflage BDU's, he watched how the sun was coloring the plains in the far distance. Now seventeen months after the devastation, there were no airplanes flying, no cars in the distance. The air was brisk and refreshing. He saw no movement, save for a few clouds near the mountains to the south.

Every time he came out he could see the difference in the air quality. At first the dust and debris blocked off the sun. He had read that a nuclear winter would last for years, but the massive storms that raged for months all over the world cleared up most of it. If it had not been almost winter when it happened, most of the plant life would have died. The area he was in had received very little radiation.

Still pondering, the slightest sound caught his attention. Patient and unmoving, he saw a fat rabbit moving along a small game trail. His snare was simple but effective. As the rabbit walked through the noose, it tightened around its neck. The frightened rabbit jumped and squirmed, but the noose held tight. Approaching quietly, he quickly grabbed the rabbit by the back legs and ears and stretched. The neck snapped quietly. He removed the snare, put it in his pocket, and walked away from the trail. He did not want any death scent around the trail. He stopped briefly, looked at the rabbit and thanked it for its life. When he first came out to hunt, it almost made him ill to take the life of such innocent creatures. In time it was not so bad. Sometimes when he came upon a trap, and an animal was still twitching, he hated what he had to do. To leave it to suffer was not something he could do.

After a few minutes, he reached a tree where, laying his bow on the ground, he tied the hind legs to a branch. He cut around each ankle, down the inside of each leg to the anus and started pulling the skin down. He made a cut around the neck and separated the skin from the animal. Next he made a cut up the center of the hide. It would be tanned using the brains soon. Cutting carefully around the anus, he then pulled the intestines away from the carcass. He cut the esophagus and pulled everything out. He separated the heart, liver and most of the intestines. The intestines would be cleaned, dried and used for sewing animal skins together. He opened the brain case carefully, dug out the brains and put them in a small plastic bag, then buried the rest of the remains in the hard dirt.

As he stood up, he saw two men standing not more than seventy five feet from him. His movement caught the attention of one of them.

Wayne froze, watching for their reaction.

The other turned to look, and both watched him for a second. As they eyed each other, Wayne inched closer to a nearby tree.

The one that had first seen him, suddenly pulled out a pistol and fired two shots.

Wayne bolted behind the tree, free of any injury. He smoothly un-shouldered his rifle, thumbed the safety off, and brought it into firing position on the other side of the Aspen.

He saw the second man limping out of sight. Not wasting any time, he quickly stepped back over, picked up his bow and started backing up. He went several yards when another shot rang out, this time from his right. He felt a tug on his coat as a bullet ripped through it. He turned and ran deeper into a growth of small evergreen trees. A second later, another shot rang out nearly a hundred and forty degrees from the other direction. They were trying to out flank him.

During the harsh winter months, he had kept in shape by running the steps in the shelter. Now the conditioning paid off as he put on some speed, zig-zagging behind the stubby evergreens.

Instead of heading straight to the shelter, he turned ninety degrees to his previous route. After a few minutes, he made another ninety degree turn, trying to outflank *them*.

He slowed down to a slow walk and quieted his breathing, taking everything in with a heightened sense reality.

He kneeled down by a tree when he figured he was close to where he thought the first man was. With his breathing under control, he waited.

Less than a minute later the first one to take a shot at him slowly stood up and walked from behind a budding bush.

Wayne waited patiently as the man walked slowly across his field of vision. He would be out of sight within twenty feet. He thumbed off the safety and took aim. He took a deep breath in, then half way out he held it. The old British rifle had open sights but was fairly accurate at this distance. He slowly squeezed the trigger. A split second before the rifle recoiled the man stumbled over something, causing the bullet to graze a shoulder blade.

Wayne was immediately up and running in a crouch. This time he was heading directly away from the shelter. He could almost feel his back tingle in anticipation of a bullet hitting him, but he did not hear any more shots and was truly thankful.

With two armed men hunting him, he was not going to take any more chances. He put distance between them as best that he could. The rugged landscape soon took its toll, and he had to slow to a walk. He did not want to kill that man, but was somewhat disappointed at missing him.

After circling around for nearly an hour, Wayne cautiously made his way toward the shelter. He stopped often and just stood, waiting and listening. The sun was well over the edge of the mountains as he watched for any activity. He figured that by now, leading them away from his property; they were long gone.

Taking a deep breath of the fresh morning air, he felt strangely relaxed and happy. The sadness of humanity destroying itself eased every time he came outside. Even though the incident with the two men disturbed him, he felt secure in his surroundings. This was his element and nothing felt better than being where he was. He felt so alive!

He walked for another half mile, stopped and lifted his binoculars. He saw something flying way out on the horizon. Even with the binoculars he was not sure what it was. He lowered them and walked up the side of a hill, stopping and watching for any movement. There were trees planted on the hill to make it look natural. In reality, it was the buried shelter. Crouching and moving slowly so as not to draw any eyes, he moved slowly up to the top. A three-foot rock stuck up from the grass where he stopped. A similar rock jutted up from scraggly dead grass about twelve feet to the other side. Again, he was extraordinarily patient and just watched for any movement. The sun was warming his face as he reached down beside the rock, pulled a lever and lifted the hollow fiberglass and metal shell up. He stepped down several steps, closed and secured the latch, then continued down several more feet. There was another latch at the bottom of the shaft, which opened as he approached it. The heat rising from the two story underground structure was almost stifling after being in the cold, fresh air for a few hours.

His wife, Perra, was waiting for him as usual. A very dedicated wife, she always waited with some apprehension when her husband left the shelter. In her hands, she had a wind up dosimeter. It was extremely rare and, in fact, made just for the couple. The few clicks it emitted reassured them both that the rabbit and the man was safe from radiation poisoning.

He handed her the rabbit, organs and brains and turned back to re-secure the metal cover.

They were not in any way low on food, but their stores got boring after a few months, so the occasional foray to spice up their food supply was almost a necessity.

"Did you see anything, honey ko?" asked his Filipino wife in her high-pitched voice.

Gazing down into her big brown eyes, he knew that she was asking about people, airplanes, anything. Growing up in the Philippines, she knew what a hard life was about, but the emergency preparedness of her husband was beyond her experience. After she arrived in the U.S., she had a terribly difficult time accepting that the one place many of her countrymen wanted to go to was now destroyed. Her anguish at losing touch with her family in her native country still lasted, and would for a long time.

"I had a run in with a couple of guys, but I lost them," he said down playing what had happened. "Beside that, I only saw this rabbit, a few squirrels and maybe an eagle."

The alarm that crept into her expressive eyes, as she looked up at her husband, had been predictable. She coiled several strands of hair with her right hand, without thinking about it.

"Are you okay?" She asked immediately.

"Of course," he said with a smile.

She hated it when he went out alone. After a long hug, she muttered, "I'd better get this rabbit into some water."

He knew her dreams of a better life died along with millions of people on that fateful day. They knew that their love was the best thing both of them had ever had, and even though life was irrevocably changed, they were still happy to be together.

The cold mountain water and some salt would keep the rabbit until night, when Perra could cook it without anyone seeing the smoke from the fire.

The lack of light did not bother them now as much as it did the first few months. They had small lights that ran off the 12-volt batteries. It did not take long to get used to the dark, but usually they slept the dark hours away and woke up with the light filtering in from the light tubes. At night, they kept a single light lit in the bathroom, for convenience, and to make their home feel less like a tomb.

The walls were of concrete that had been treated with waterproofing, and then had thick plastic laid over it before the dirt. Somehow it always seemed dank and stuffy.

It did not bother them much to wait for the solar heater to warm the mountain water enough for them to shower. The hardest part was to use the hand pump and get enough water for the heater. After they finished pumping they would switch the water line back, so others could use it for the sinks and toilet. Within a few hours they could take a nice hot shower.

At first they heated food using propane, but that soon ran low, so they only ate one hot meal per day. It was best to use a small fire at night when nobody could see the smoke. They disguised the chimney like an old tree trunk. Anybody that could smell it, if anyone were still around, would have a very hard time tracking where it originated.

The four air vents angled up at different directions to provide fresh air. No matter what direction the wind came from, there was always some suction in one direction, and fresh air coming from another. On calm days, they had a 12-volt fan they could use to draw in fresh air. Readily available was a back up hand crank that would also bring in the life-giving air. Attached just before the hand pump was a removable nuclear, biological and chemical filter. A few times during the night the carbon dioxide monitor went off, making everyone scramble to fix the problem. All they had to do was pop open both of the escape hatches. The warmer air upstairs would rise, pulling in cool, fresh air in from the vents.

Going down the right set of stairs he automatically checked the hinges to the metal cover. It could be locked from below or above, just in case their hideout got breached. In the dank environment, the hinges could get rusty. That too was something he had planned for. He had kept a few gallons of used motor oil to keep the hinges from locking up.

After inspecting the hinges, he stopped briefly and looked around at his creation. The time he had spent drawing up the plans had been well worth the effort. There was hardly a day that went by that he did not notice what he had accomplished. He originally wished that he had more money for a better layout, but as he scanned his home, it just felt right. The upstairs was not only the kitchen and dining room it was the library. There were hundreds of books and games lining the far wall, opposite from the escape hatches, sink and hand water pump.

As he went down the stairs, he could feel the air get cooler. He could see fairly well, even though he just came from outside a minute before. The two light tubes that ran from just above the ground to the lower inside living area were bringing in as much light as a 25-watt bulb. At the bottom, he turned left, then went several feet and made another left into the bathroom. He did not like defecating or urinating outside. No matter how good you buried it, something was going to smell it. He tried to leave the least amount of human smell as he could. He did not want to scare off anything that might be needed for survival.

After using the toilet, he cleaned up and made a left, and then another left, so he could put up the rifle and bow and arrows. He unloaded the 1942 British .303 and put it back in its place. Then he hung up the compound bow. Even though it was the "armory", they did not keep it locked. To the right were the many 12-volt batteries, many assorted replacement parts and other electronics. The batteries were designed for golf carts. When he bought them, the salesman said that they would last ten to 12 years.

"Up again early Wayne?" His older brother Dane asked sleepily. Turning around, he could see between the hanging sheets of his room. Dane was not in very good shape these days, although he was in better shape now than a year ago. Before the fall, Dane had been on a few medications for Bipolar disorder. Now, with much more attention to proper nutrition, his mood swings had improved a lot.

There were very few preservatives in the food he ate now. Gone were the refined sugars, flours, the additives, the genetically modified foods, the addictive ingredients, the fillers and the dyes. Also gone were the pesticides, hormones, pollutants and radiation. It thoroughly pissed Wayne off whenever he thought of the greedy bastards, and the filthy scum sucking FDA that allowed all of that junk to be put into humanities food. He was glad they were all gone.

"Yes, I went out to get some fresh meat. You should try to go with me next time. It's awesome out there. The snow's gone, and everything is just starting to bloom. It's surprising to see how clear the air is now.

Lying his head back down on his pillow, he said, "Yeah, I'd like that. Maybe I'll go with you next time."

Dane was dreadfully pale from being out of the sun for so long. He normally loved being outside, helping to trap and hunt, but lately he just slept a lot. When he got up, he tried to help out, but kept getting tired. When he got tired, he got grumpy. When he was grumpy it was miserable to be around him, so he usually read or slept.

"Well, it's probably not too safe out there right now. I had a run in with a couple of guys, and I don't think they will be leaving the area any time soon." He told him of the incident and showed him the bullet hole in his coat.

"You got lucky," Dane said.

"Yeah, and if they don't leave, and we can't get rid of them, we may need to find help."

"They were tough, huh?"

"They seemed to know what they were doing. One of them had a bad limp, so he couldn't go very fast. It was the other one that I went after first."

"I don't think it's a good idea for you go out by yourself anymore."

"I was thinking the same thing," said Wayne.

"You realized that they may find us."

"Yes, which leaves us three choices, stay and fight, leave and find another place, or try and find other people to help us."

Tired though he was Dane was fully awake now.

"If there are two, there may be more of them."

"Yes, damn it. This is the one situation I was afraid of too, but it is what it is, and we need to figure out what to do."

The two brothers said nothing as they pondered their plight.

"Let me sleep on it." Dane laid his head back down on his pillow.

Heading back to his room, Wayne sat on the bed and took off his boots. He put on the soft moccasin shoes his wife made for him. He went back up the stairs and nuzzled his wife's neck as she was preparing his breakfast. She always got goose bumps when he breathed on her neck. He had always liked that about her and loved to take advantage of it when he could.

Breathing in deeply and exhaling through pursed lips, she put the spoon down and tapped on her left arm. "Oh honey ko! I'll jump you right here!" She said quietly.

Their lovemaking was seldom due to the thin sheet walls and lack of privacy. Once in a while they would escape into the false mini bunker and have at it, but with the spring time upon them they could escape for some fun in the sun. He would just have to make sure he did not get a sun burn on his "very white butt", as his wife called it.

She put a bowl of almost hot cereal on the table. She used some of the precious propane to heat just a little water for his breakfast. It was getting warm enough outside that now when he came back in, she would not need to make him anything to warm him up.

Although he missed butter on his cereal, he took a bite, smiled and told her how good it was.

"I think I might have seen something out there."

Perra looked up from her meal suddenly. Her whole body seemed to be radiating the question he knew she wanted to ask.

"Just before I came back, I saw... something... way out there. It could have been an eagle. Whatever it was, it appeared to be gliding. I didn't hear anything, but that doesn't mean much at the distance it was."

"Do you think it could have been an airplane?" She asked as her big brown eyes sought out every movement of his face and eyes.

"Maybe, but I'm just not sure."

"Oh honey ko, I hope so."

"I wasn't even going to mention it, but since I had a run in with those two guys we may have to leave. It's either that or stay and fight them if they find us."

The quick turn of the conversation put a confused look on Perra's face.

"Leave? We can't leave, we don't have a place to go!" She all but cried. "This is our home! There has to be another way!

"Well, we do have some options as far as where to go. Our only other choice is to go find other people to help us out. Either way, our time here may end.

He saw the fear in her eyes as he remembered the last time he and Dane went out. It was last fall, and Wayne was almost killed. The knife had almost sliced all the way through his coat. Fortunately for him Dane had the rifle and dropped the crazed man. Autumn had been so beautiful that he got careless and did not see the stranger coming. He had only been out three times since then, and each time he had been alone.

"Do you think those men are still around?"

"Yes, I'm sure they are still out there somewhere. I also think that there are good people out there holed up just like we are. I saw a place on the computer several years ago with a nice place that is hidden underground and was well stocked. There are Arks all over the Rocky Mountains, the Appalachians, the Tetons and the Cascades. I've also seen pictures of old silos that have been converted to bomb shelters."

"You think so?"

"Sweetheart, I know so."

"Do you think my family in the Philippines are okay?" She asked for the hundredth time.

"I think they're fine. There may have been some radioactive fall out, but they are so isolated that, by the time the wind got there, most of the fall out was probably diluted. Besides, they had no enemies, so they should have been safe."

"I still miss them very much, honey ko." She said as a tear slid down her face.

"I know sweetheart. It tears me up not knowing about my family too." He suddenly straightened. "It's time we start to find out though. We've been locked up in here for long enough. I'm sure that there are friendly people out there, and are trying to find people like us. After breakfast, we can get out the radio and see if anyone is on the air." They usually tried once a month to see if anyone were broadcasting, but so far they heard nothing. They had protected the wind up radio by wrapping it in a box, which was then wrapped with aluminum foil. He had just wrapped it up several months before it happened.

"Oh honey ko, you think so? Can we start looking for other people? Maybe they have better radios. I really do hope we can find someone else to talk to soon. Do you think we will be able to talk to anyone in the Philippines?"

"I don't know sweetheart. If anyone can talk to someone in the Philippines, it will probably be someone from a government agency, if they are still around. Maybe there's someone with a ham radio that was smart enough to protect it."

"But first, we will have to be very careful of those two guys I met. They aren't very happy right now."

"Oh honey ko, you need to be very careful out there!" She said with concern in her voice.

"Don't worry, sweetheart. We'll take precautions. Anyway," he said to steer her away from the topic of the two men, "don't get your hopes up. The first thing we need to do is check the radio, then start doing a lot of walking. We'll have to make sure the area is clear before we get too comfortable outside. It may take a few months before we are ready to go very far. We just can't be too cautious."

"Oh honey ko, I'm so excited. I know it will take a while before we know anything, but at least we have a goal now. It's something different from the same thing every day."

Dane seemed to come alive with the news, and agreed that it was time to do something besides lay around waiting to die.

By lunch, they agreed to some rules to being outside: One person would always be near the shelter and ready to provide cover for the other two, should they be in trouble. All of them would be armed. They would only go out for one hour, heading in a prearranged direction for a half hour before returning. They would carry small mirrors to communicate so as not to draw any attention to themselves. The two searchers would not lose sight of each other, and would keep a reasonable distance from each other to cover more area. If one of them should be caught by any hostiles, the other was to get away as quietly as possible and return to the shelter. If possible, observe where the other was held, count how many hostiles there are, what living conditions, and how many weapons they have. No food would be taken out of the shelter, since the smell could attract unwanted attention. They would skirt any open areas and stay to the trees and bushes.

For the first time in many months, they stayed up late talking of different scenarios and possibilities, both good and bad. The biggest thing they had to consider was that Dane and Perra were used to being inside and not used to very much travel or sun, hence the short trips out and back. The next thing they considered was that safety was paramount. The need for stealth was extremely high. The last thing they talked about was if both the searchers did not come back. That would put a terribly heavy burden on the person whose turn it was to stay behind. They agreed just before they turned in for the night that the person staying back would wait an extra hour, then head inside, wait another hour, then set out with food, water and medical supplies and try to locate the others.

They were excited to have something to do besides eat, sleep, and read. As a result, they did not get much sleep. Many scenarios kept going through their minds as they envisioned the unknown lands around them. They all knew that the land had been sparsely populated due to the large tracts of land where they and their neighbors lived. Even then, the tracts of land had been in rugged country located 10 miles from the nearest town, making it very slim that anyone would be around. Anyone except for the two killers.

CHAPTER 2
MINIONS

The two cousins had made the journey to Colorado to hunt elk. Neither one had been particularly educated or smart, but they were skilled hunters. Their camp had been deep in the woods and exceptionally well hidden. They hid it because they were poachers. They killed whatever they could for fun, as well as for food. They did not use rifles, due to the noise. They preferred the latest in compound bows, which could easily cost a couple thousand dollars.

When the weather suddenly changed and plunged them into a blustery winter darkness, they decided it was time to go home. They packed up their gear and prepared for the long drive home, but the truck would not start. The mountain top they had chosen was directly in line with one of the over lapping zones of EMP, but they did not know that. Even if they did, they probably would not have understood it in any case. So rather than get stranded on top of a mountain during the winter months, they decided to hike out to the nearest town. They figured it was a few days away, even with the rough terrain and quickly changing weather.

Four days later they stumbled, half frozen and thirsty, into a small town by a reservoir. The place was a mess and people were fighting all over the place. They decided to hide in a small cabin set back from the small town and wait it out. Dried food was abundant. An inside water pump, along with plenty of canned food, was just waiting for them to use. They dared not use the wood stove. They were not that stupid.

The weather continued to get worse, and more than a few trees fell around the sturdy log cabin.

After a few weeks, the turmoil below them had mostly stopped. It was time to go find out what was going on, and decided it would be best if they went without their bows. It was the only thing that saved their lives.

Fresh graves littered the area, as well as burned out vehicles of all sorts. It looked like a war zone, and made the two men unusually nervous. Heavy wind, dark skies and heavy, dirty rain blanketed the area on and off. The wind was unrelenting. Still, they approached several men that had been scavenging parts from a truck. They came down through the trees until they could be seen, then held their hands up to show the men that they were unarmed. A few of the men picked up weapons and trained them on the strangers. They let the two men approach, and a slender figure approached them.

A man with a wild look, sporting a fresh cut lip and a broken tooth, quizzed them quickly. Their skills, he said, would benefit "The Blessed Mother", whoever that was. To prove themselves, they would need to bring in fresh meat for the people. A day later the men brought in a large fresh elk. They were soon accepted into the small community, and their job was to continue bringing in fresh meat. A few weeks later they got appointed a new task: find and bring in females of breeding age.

Although part of the new community, they thought the Boss was crazy. Still, they did as they were told and found a few survivors here and there. As a reward, they had each been given a young woman for a night. It had something to do with spreading their seed for a new world. Empowered, they renewed their search. This time, however, they felt that they could get away with taking what they wanted. The Boss did not need to know. So they ranged further, staying out days at a time, sometimes for a week or more. They grew overly bold and started having fun, killing, torturing and raping at will. Still, they produce the occasional woman or girl unharmed.

They almost paid the ultimate price when a red-headed woman surprised them. She had shot them both. One took a bullet in the knee. The other one lost a piece of his ear. They had barely made it out alive. They decided pay closer attention after they ran into the last person. They were sure they could get the drop on him, but he quickly disappeared into the trees. Try as they could, they could only track him for a short way. They decided it was time to get out of the area when he grazed the should blade on one of them. With such a dangerous man around, it was time to get their gear and head back to the safety of the community. Let the Boss deal with him.

CHAPTER 3
BOUNTY

At sunlight Wayne, Perra and Dane got up and readied their weapons and gear. Breakfast was canned chicken mixed with rice, coffee and homemade oat squares with honey.

Although she felt excited at the prospect of getting out and doing something, Perra decided to stay near the shelter first. She drew fresh water for the canteens and handed them to the two guys as they climbed the latter. She had a smaller jug of water and binoculars with her as she anxiously climbed up after them. She kept to herself the fact that she felt terrified that the two strangers would find her by herself.

The crisp morning was calm and quiet. The two men slowly emerged from the shelter, followed by Perra. The sun was barely above the horizon but did not reach them through the trees. All three of them just sat there for several moments as they took in the scents and views. The pine smell was almost overwhelming at first, but after a few minutes they could detect other scents mixed in, as well.

Perra tugged her coat tighter around her as she looked around for the first time in months. The last time she had been outside, her husband was almost slashed with a knife, and just yesterday met two mean people. She had felt so secure in the shelter and outside had come to mean "bad". Now that she was outside with the guys, she felt exposed but safe. She felt some vertigo since there was no longer a roof as a point of reference. In a few moments, the vertigo passed and she felt her spirits lifting again.

They synchronized their watches. They were all wind up watches, bought from an antique dealer years before.

"Are you sure you don't want to go on the first trip Perra," Dane asked, who stood looking out between the trees.

"No thanks, I'll just sit here and use the binoculars. Please be safe, guys. Remember, one hour. You won't be gone longer than that, will you?"

"No sweetheart," said Wayne, "we should be back before then, just to make sure you are all right," said her husband.

"I'll be alright, honey ko. Just don't take too long, okay?"

"Ok, sweetheart. If you see those guys get inside as fast as you can and lock the hatch."

They hugged and then quietly the two men headed down the grassy hill. Their direction was toward the nearest house, about a mile distant. The sparsely wooded hills allowed them to walk about a hundred feet apart. The wind picked up slightly as they made their way slowly in the direction of the house. Neither of them believed the owners were still alive. The semi retired couple had lived in Denver and had only come out occasionally. On the rare occasion that he saw his neighbor, they would chat for a long time about the condition of the world and how everything was falling apart. The house seemed hidden from the road, but anyone walking a hundred and fifty yards onto the property would find it.

Rounding a hill, they slowed down. They had prearranged hand signals for stop, look, danger, all clear and retreat. Dane was holding up his left hand for stop as a sound came from a hundred feet ahead. They slowly crouched down next to the nearest tree. Something was moving, but the trees that afforded them shelter also blocked them from seeing just what it was.

The breeze shifted direction, and suddenly the slight noise quickly became hoofs pounding through the grass and shrubs. Within seconds, the sound died.

Dane was the better woodsman and the better shot, so he again made the "stop" sign. He slowly went forward and intersected a game trail that went in their general direction. He came back a few minutes later and signed the "all clear" signal.

They approached the trail and could see the prints from at least two deer. The old man and his wife had planted a variety of plants, bushes and trees that the deer evidently found tasty.

"At least we know there's big game still around," said Dane.

Wayne nodded agreement.

They could see the house now, and could see that the window on the front door was broken. The solar panels on the roof looked a little dirty, but were not broken that they could see. As they got closer, they could see the front door slightly ajar. Dane was visibly tiring so his younger brother slowly approached. Dane had his weapon up and ready.

Taking his time and breathing slowly, Wayne approached the smallest window on the side of the house. He figured that if people were inside, they would have come out when the deer took off. It suddenly occurred to him that they heard them and took cover. Unruffled, he took his time and took out his small inspection mirror. He slowly moved it around, so he could peek inside.

The house was not in too bad of shape. Someone evidently ransacked the place, but they did not cause too much damage. It even looked like they stayed there for a while. *They probably stayed until the food ran out; and then went to look for more*, he thought.

He eased up to another window and again, could see just a slightly mussed up room. Taking his time, he went up to the front door and slipped inside. He did so without moving the door.

Dane was watching intently as Wayne disappeared inside the doorway.

Wayne almost had a heart attack as a bird flew out the broken window on the door.

Quickly getting his breath back, Dane moved up to the door and peeked inside. The dust on the hardwood floor showed only small prints. Wayne was just inside the door with a white face.

"Damn bird scared the crap out of me," he whispered.

"It looks like it's been deserted for a long time, but lets check out the back door and see if anyone has been coming and going from there," said Dane.

They back-tracked and went around the back. The door was intact and closed. There was no sign of prints or of anyone being there for a long time. They entered slowly and again saw just small prints on the floor.

"When the Marshall's were building this house I showed them the shelter. They were so impressed that they modified their plans and put in a secret shelter too. I guess it pissed off their contractor, but they didn't care since they had the extra money to spend. It's a lot smaller than ours, and I know how to get into it."

"Why didn't you tell me?" Dane asked.

"If you'd been caught I didn't want that info to fall into the hands of anyone else. I'd planned as their shelter being our back up in case our place gets compromised. I didn't even tell Perra. She knew that they were adding another room, but not a reinforced shelter. John Marshall was a hunter in his day. He said he was going to load up with weapons, ammo and food. He told me that if shit hit the fan and he never made it back, that we could take what we want. If anyone else got the same message, today is the day to find out."

"Cool," was all Dane managed to say before Wayne headed down the hallway.

Turning left into the kitchen they passed a few open cupboards. Dane tried the propane stove and jumped when it lit. Evidently the solar panels still worked.

"Whoever stayed here, at least, had the decency to save some propane."

Wayne walked over and opened the pantry door. Surprisingly, the light automatically came on as he did so.

Going to the back of the pantry, which was empty, he lifted off four shelves and laid them aside. He pulled the upper left shelf bracket and part of the wood paneled back wall swung open. A few small LED lights came on inside, as well.

"Damn, that's cool," Dane said.

They headed down the narrow staircase, which had a wall about four feet away from the landing. The wall was of concrete blocks and had a small hole in it, about nine inches by nine inches. There were several small lights in the ceiling-enough to light up the room. They just stood in shocked awe, as they took in the bounty in front of them.

"Son of a….."

"Yeah," said Wayne.

They just both stood there slowly swinging their heads back and forth looking over everything. The five hundred square foot room was so full that there was just enough room to move about in the isles leading in different directions. They could not see a kitchen, bathroom or even a sleeping area.

Within a second of each other, their watches beeped, signaling that their time was half over.

"I guess John wasn't kidding when he said he was going to stock up on supplies. It makes our supplies look like dinner for two," said Dane.

The two men reluctantly turned around and went back up the concrete steps. Wayne closed the secret door, reset the shelves then closed the pantry door.

Although they tried to concentrate on their trip back, they kept seeing all of the boxes of dried food, the packages of pudding, the MREs, the bottled water, and boxes of chocolate. John and his wife had been heavy, but Wayne did not suspect that they had such a sweet tooth. Just from where they could see there had to have been hundreds of boxes of food and supplies. Wayne had stocked a few boxes of comfort foods, but nothing like what he had just seen.

The water, and what looked like cider, had been stored in glass and not plastic. There were boxes of dried jerky, potatoes, milk, eggs and spices. They even saw some home-canned meat of some sort. All in all they could only see about ten percent of what was there, considering it was stacked almost to the ceiling.

Damn, thought Wayne. *I knew we should have tried this earlier.*

They reached their hidden bunker with several minutes to spare. Perra was not visible, and Wayne's heart skipped a beat. As they approached cautiously, she appeared from inside a pine tree.

"Sorry honey ko, I had to pee." She said sheepishly.

Suddenly Wayne scooped her up and swung her around in a circle.

"Honey ko!" She squealed.

"We found a large cache of food and supplies at John and Linda's place. We didn't have time to check it out, but the place is full. We'll have to go back and check it out better. We could live off all of that food for years!" Wayne said with a huge smile.

"Oh, I'm so glad, but you didn't see anyone?" She asked in her little girl voice.

"Nobody's been there for a long time," Dane said from behind her. "Unless you want to count the bird that scared the crap out of us." Wayne added with a smile.

They all laughed as they headed back into the shelter. It suddenly seemed very closed in and stuffy.

As Perra made lunch, they talked of the find and what to do next. As much as they wanted to go rifling through the goodies, they decided that the hidden cache could wait until they were sure the surrounding hills were safe. They talked briefly of moving into the other shelter, but they were settled in here, and the other place was still a big unknown.

By nightfall, they were all still excited but tired. Dane did not look too good, but the life had finally come back in his eyes.

CHAPTER 4
REVULSION

The next day Dane decided to stay back. The local map showed dirt roads going all over, and for miles. They marked the houses as well as they could remember on the map. The houses were still their best bet for finding people, although after so long, they doubted anyone would still be out here. They settled on the next closest house, which was on the same ridge as their home, but on top. They would approach from a game trail Wayne knew went up the side of the hill. This time they would leave before sunrise, just in case anyone could see them walking up toward the house. They would have to take a chance at being seen on the way back down.

For the hundredth time, Wayne wished he had built on top of the ridge and built the shelter down in the hard shale. He could have made look-outs from inside the shelter, so they could see the eastern plains easier. On the down side, they would have had to drill another hundred feet to get to water.

Dressed in her camouflage clothes, Perra looked out of place. They were a few sizes too big for her. Despite that, Wayne's heart swelled with pride. She had come from an extremely poor country, moved to a wealthy one, then ended up in much harder times than she ever had back home. At times her child-like reaction to new things made her seem so naive, but her determination and dedication to her husband and her life were what made her strong. At times, she seemed so fragile, but her toughness came out at the most unexpected times.

Perra had gotten up early and made a quick breakfast. They were all ready a full hour before the sun was up. This time they were planning on taking an hour and a half, just to make sure they had time to get up the hill and down again.

Dane grumbled a little bit when he spilled hot coffee on his hand as he was finishing his breakfast.

They headed North West toward the game trail, this time with Wayne leading the way. He had his wife stay about a hundred feet back. She wanted to walk with him, but he insisted she stay back to cover him in case he got in trouble. He hoped that if something happened, and she had to fire a shot to scare someone away, that she would not shoot him. She was scared of guns and was a horrible shot.

The moon was still up and provided just enough light for them to see the way. The sun was not due to be up for a while yet, but the eastern sky was getting lighter by the minute.

Twenty minutes later they were at the base of the ridge. The game trail followed the easiest route up, and it was still wet from the morning dew. He located a secure spot, and waited for his wife to catch up. He decided that the best way to go was to leap frog their way up. He would go up a few yards, stop and make sure he saw no one, then have her do the same.

They reached the top after several minutes, then rested for a short while.

"Are you okay, sweetheart?" He asked her.

"Oh yes, I'm okay. My legs are a little tired. I wish I would have exercised for a while before doing this."

"I felt that too. My legs are still a little bit sore from yesterday. The house is about a hundred yards along the ridge. We should stay well away from the edge, so we don't show a silhouette."

"I'll just take some water, and then I'll be ready," she said.

After another minute, Wayne set off again. He slowed down considerably as the house came into view.

The sun was almost up to the horizon as he approached the side of the house. The garage was on his side of the house, so he was not too worried about anyone seeing him from inside. He tried the side door and found it unlocked. He slowly opened it and saw that the garage door was wide open. No cars were inside. Debris was several inches deep in places. He did not see any foot prints, so he waved Perra to come up to him.

"So far it seems abandoned. Let's go in slow and quiet. Once the house is clear we'll see if there is anything useful still here."

With weapons low, they entered the pantry. It was empty of course, so they slowly and quietly headed through the kitchen looking for the bedrooms. They made no noise as they crept along the carpet. They froze as a board creaked under Wayne's foot. It seemed an eternity before he slowly lifted his foot and went forward again. Perra carefully stepped around the noisy spot.

The place was dusty but not in bad shape. Wayne could see his tidy wives' mind turning as she was almost tempted to start wiping away the dust. He turned away with a smile on his face.

As they went through the living room, they went passed several family pictures on the wall. The mother and daughter were almost splitting images of each other. The littlest one, a boy, was about four. They went up some stairs and down a hall way. A few of the doors were open, with no sign that anyone had been there in a long time. Wayne went into the first room on the right as his wife went down the hall. He looked at the posters of handsome young men on the wall and turned to look at the colorful bedspread. *Poor girl*, he thought.

A blood-curdling scream came from his wife as he whipped around and sped out of the room, while bringing his rifle up. He did not see her at first but could hear her sobs as he closed in on her in no time. She had dropped her weapon and had her hands to her face. She froze in place and could not tear her eyes away from the master bed.

Wayne stepped in front of her immediately to shield her from the desiccated body there. The brief look he had told the story. The red headed woman lay stretched out naked, with her throat cut. Undoubtedly she had been raped before being brutally killed. Her wrinkled up skin told the story of a sharp knife slashing in several places, beside her throat. Dried blood was everywhere. The dried up orbs in her sockets seem to stare at both of them.

"Come on sweetheart, you don't need to see that."

He picked up the fallen rifle and walked his wife out of the room. He closed the door and turned to hold his wife for a few minutes.

"I want to go back now, honey ko." She said in a pitiful voice.

"I want to get out of here too Perra, but there may be a small chance that there is a ham radio here. I saw an antenna sticking up from the roof when we approached. If it's still in decent shape, we could probably hook it up at John and Linda's place. The solar panels are still producing electricity.

"I want to go...."

"It will only take a minute, then we can leave," he said.

She simply nodded her head and moved further down the hall, away from the grisly scene.

He slowly opened the next door across the hall and found it empty, except for some craft supplies. He had to kick in the next door since it was locked. He figured that if anyone were around they would have heard the scream and been on them by now, so being quiet now was a waste of time. Thinking he found the ham radio room he stepped in without a thought. He nearly froze in mid-step as he confronted another horrifying scene.

It looked as if the father had been roughed up, tied up and executed while on his knees. Just before Wayne stepped back out of the room, he saw a small pair of feet on the other side of the bed. He almost vomited then, but wanted to stay strong for his wife. He controlled his face as best as he could as he re-emerged into the hallway and closed the door.

"The radio's not in there," he managed.

The next room back toward the living room was closed but unlocked. It was opposite the first room he entered. He found what he was looking for, or what was left of it. The metal baseball bat was still sticking out of the bent and broken metal casing of the radio. Whoever destroyed it must have been pissed off because they had a way to communicate, but no power.

The senseless of it all came back in a rush. His first impulse was to burn this house of misery. These senseless deaths, pain and misery, were a bitter reminder of what "civilized" men had become. Hate and war, greed and murder, culminated from thousands of years of so-called civilization, and look what society had become. This only reconfirmed his life long belief that there was no god. *The Knights Templars were right,* he thought, *Christianity was faked. It was just another tool to control people. What better way to raise a faithful and dedicated society? What better way to create fighting forces that would die willingly for their cause?*

Perra could see into the room from where she was in the hallway. Wayne did not think her face could have fallen any more, yet she managed it somehow.

They had such high hopes after yesterdays find. Today was just the opposite. They hated what they found. It was time to leave.

They headed back out to the living room. Wayne decided to take a quick peek down the stairs in what was probably the family room. It was evident that the person or people took their time here. He could see a bunch of soda cans, beer cans and food wrappers. There was a big-screen television on the far wall. As he entered, he saw a couch on the right, which folded out into a hide-a-bed. On it, he found the young girl whose room was just above him. Rage boiled in him as he looked at her desiccated nude body. She could not have been more than twelve or thirteen. She laid tied up and spread-eagled on the bed. She too had been raped, but she did not die by knife. It looked like they used her until the food ran out, and then broke her neck.

This time he *did* retch. He quickly backed away and almost fell going up the steps. His wife knew something went terribly wrong down there, and could not wait to leave. She slung her rifle over her shoulder as she ran back out the way they came. She briefly looked over her shoulder to see if her husband was following.

Wayne felt as if he were suffocating until he broke free of the house. He ran after his wife, who seemed to be faster than him at the moment.

He caught up to her at the game trail, where they collapsed. It was just too much. They lay there gasping for air for several minutes. Wayne's watch alarm went off, and a few seconds later so did Perra's.

They did not speak at all on the way back to the shelter. Wayne did not care if anyone heard them. He wanted someone to try and stop him. *Please*, he thought. *Show your fucking face so I can blow it off!* After several minutes, he calmed down and realized that not everyone left alive would be his enemy.

He suddenly had a sinking feeling that the two men that had come after him may have killed the family, and that was extremely concerning. It meant that they had been in the area for a long time, and did not want to leave.

Dane was watching them with the binoculars when they came into sight of the shelter. He could tell something was wrong by the defeated and weary way they walked. Something went seriously wrong today.

The brothers made eye contact and understood that they would talk about it later. After taking a nice, warm shower, and drinking some of their dwindling coffee, Wayne told his older brother all about the trip.

"I figured something like that must have happened all over the place, but I didn't think it would happen to our neighbors," Dane said quietly. "They deserve a burial."

"I'd thought of that on the way home, but I can't go back

there for a while. Maybe we can go in a few days, or a week at most, but not now. Perra's going to be useless for a few days at least. She may not even want to go out and keep watch while we're gone. Right now she needs the routine of being in familiar surroundings."

Dane reflected on the recent happenings for a moment.

"She took it really hard, didn't she?" He asked needlessly.

"Yes, but at least she didn't see the little girl. She had a niece in the Philippines about her age when the bombs fell. That would have really devastated her had she seen her. That's the first time in my life I've thrown up without the help of alcohol. Speaking of which, I think I need some. Do you want any?"

"No thanks, maybe later."

Nothing more was said for most of the day. Perra took a shower, slept for a while, and prepared their lunch, then dinner.

Wayne approached her when she was cleaning the dinner dishes and held her from behind. She turned around, clung to him and quietly sobbed. Wayne joined her as they released the pent up feelings and frustration.

For the next two days, they stayed inside. Dane grumbled and paced, but stayed inside. Surprisingly, it was Perra that went out first.

She had brooded for those two days in silent misery. The third day she was up early, made breakfast and announced that they needed to bury the bodies.

"Sweetheart, the area isn't clear. We don't know if those slime bags are still around. We..."

"Let them come, we have guns. We will make them pay!" She said with quiet vehemence.

Wayne was slightly taken aback. His peace-loving wife always seemed to surprise him, despite their six-year marriage. He had never seen this side before, but then, she had never been exposed to the carnage they had witnessed.

Dane was determined to go too. He had kept up his pacing for the last two days and occasionally would stare out of the light tubes.

Wayne wanted to get outside, but kept seeing the sunken sockets of the lady and her daughter. He hardly slept, and when he did he woke up thinking someone was there with a knife. They all needed to get done what none of them wanted to do.

Chapter 5
Return

For the first time since they entered the shelter so long ago, they all departed their hidden home together. Perra led with a shovel and a rifle slung over her shoulder. Wayne came next with his faithful 1942 British .303, a shovel, and a pick. Lastly, Dane followed with his hunting rifle, canteen and binoculars. He hung back a dozen yards, just in case.

They got to the house without stopping this time. Dane, slightly winded, stayed determined not to lose the other two.

The sun was half way up when they entered the house. Dane searched for a way on top of the roof. He would not have a better vantage point from which to keep a look out. None of the Colorado evergreen trees even came up to the eaves. He found a ladder on the back inside wall of the three car garage.

Stopping at the door, Wayne gave his wife a face mask and gloves. He donned his as he entered. He went downstairs first, so he could throw a sheet over the body of the young girl before his wife could see. He cut the cords and telephone wire from her small wrists.

They managed to wrap her up and carry her from each end of the sheet. Her remains weighed almost nothing. They set her down and went back inside to get her mother, doing the same routine.

The father was harder, since he fell on the rug and his blood congealed and stuck his skin and clothes to the carpet. Wayne had to go back out and get a shovel, so he could pry the body up. They used a blanket from the small bed to wrap him and carry him out. They laid him next to his wife.

Perra was quiet most of the time. She almost lost her nerve when they went back in for the little boy on the other side of the bed. Wayne took care of it himself as his wife stood in the hall. As Wayne carried the small bundle out, he could see the tears welling in his wife's eyes.

It took them an hour to dig into the hard soil. It was tough to get deep enough for the bodies. Dane came down from the roof when he saw how hard the dirt was to dig. By the time they completed their gruesome job, they were all winded.

Perra insisted that they find wood and make crosses for the graves. Wayne found a hammer and nails as Dane and Perra looked for some wood.

After she completed the crosses and pounded them into the soil, Perra said a few words in her native Tagalog, then in English. Wayne bowed his head in honor of the family before him. Perra's voice cracked as she muttered, "Amen."

Dane took the ladder down and put it back on the wall, then did a quick walk through of the house. He came out white as a ghost. He had a flashback of his time in the military. He kept getting flashbacks of dried blood. He was still amazed that it could be so dark.

They left and returned to their shelter in silence. After heating water and waiting their turn, they all scrubbed until their bodies were pink.

CHAPTER 6
SITTING DUCKS

They did not eat much for lunch. They went through the motions as they discussed the next place to visit. Each parcel of land was a minimum of forty acres in size. That took up a lot of ground, especially when much of the land was not yet built on yet. So they decided they were going to try to the north where they saw a few small ranches. Then they were going to head east back towards Interstate 25, where they knew more houses were located along the way. It was several miles to I-25, but they had no plans on going anywhere near the main roads yet. They would follow the dirt road from a distance and try to locate the next house. As they went, they would mark on the map the location and any other information, if any. They decided that they would leave the map at the shelter, so it would not fall into anyone else's hands.

"I think we should stay together on these outings," said Dane. "The more someone stays around up top the more the grass will be squashed down, and it feels really nice knowing that three weapons are available, instead of two," he added.

"Yes, I felt that too," said his younger brother. "I think that we should go out in a triangle pattern, with two out front and one in the back. It we do it right we should still be able to see each other."

"Yes, honey ko. I don't want to be left alone here anymore." Her lips pushed out into a slight pout.

"Are you up to walking a few miles Dane?"

"I'm tired of hiding like a rabbit," he said. "Even if I get tired, it'll be better than sitting here," he grumbled.

"Sweetheart, what about you?"

"If we can take some breaks, I'll be okay, but we need to take some food if we are going to be gone a long time."

"Ok, so, first thing in the morning we head north along the road until we find the next place."

"Do we need to get up so early? Hard telling what kinds of animals could be lurking in the dark," his brother said tiredly.

"Well, I guess we don't have to get up so early. With the sun up it won't be quite as cold. I'd feel more comfortable with more cover though."

"But there will be three of us now, instead of two," his wife pointed out.

Wayne smiled at his wife and simply said, "True."

Dane went off for a nap as Wayne and Perra stripped down the weapons, cleaned and lightly oiled them. Perra laid down for a nap too, since she had not had that much exercise in over a year.

The next morning they all rose a little stiffly. Wayne was a bit less stiff, since he kept up his routine on the stairs. They ate a leisurely breakfast with hot chocolate. The guys got their gear ready while Perra prepared a snack of peanut butter and honey on home made biscuits.

The sun was up and warming their faces as they exited the shelter. They just stood for a few minutes getting used to the light, smells and temperature. The ever vigilant Dane was using his binoculars to scan the area they were going to be heading into.

They headed off in the same general direction as the last house, but this time more to the north. The grass was just slightly damp since the sun had already been up for an hour or so. Wayne took the right front corner of the triangle, with his wife to his left and the stealthy Dane trying hard to keep them both in sight at the same time.

As they continued through thinning trees, they stopped to discuss a change in tactics. Their main cover was now starting to disappear. Dane and Wayne had on desert camouflage Battle Dress Uniforms, but Perra had on the forest pattern. She would stick out much easier on the grassy brown fields than they would.

"Oh." Perra said. "That's easy to fix. The inside is lighter than the outside. I'll just turn them inside out."

The guys just looked at each other and felt real dumb. It was an easy solution for a simple problem.

She stepped behind the bushy tree they were kneeling by and quickly changed. The clothes were almost new, and the inside colors were about half as vivid as the crisp lines of the outside. At least she would not stick out as much as before. There was nothing they could do about the dwindling trees before they headed out on the plains.

The next house appeared to be a ranch style home. Dane was checking it out with his binoculars. There was a truck slightly visible on the other side of the house and said as much to the others.

"Do you see any movement?" Whispered Perra.

Dane suddenly laughed. "No, I don't see anything but a few birds flying around."

She looked at him quizzically, and then realized that there was nobody around for at least a half mile in all directions.

"I guess I don't have to whisper then, do I?"

Dane smiled then looked back at the house, "Not yet," he replied.

The ranch house had several buildings set in different areas. There was the classical-red barn complete with hay loft and empty stables. Most of the roof appeared to be gone. One small building was probably the pump house. Another appeared to be a storage shed. Dane could just make out a small roof sticking above the ground behind the house. He figured that was a tornado shelter, even though tornados were rare in these parts of the state. All of the roofs, except for the barn, looked as if they had been recently repaired.

Wayne and Perra had their binoculars out too.

"I just saw something move in the center window on the right side of the house." Wayne said quickly.

"I thought I saw something too, honey ko."

With the house shaped in a backward "L", the long part of the L faced south. Their approach was from a north-west direction.

All three of them focused their attention on the window for a minute. They realized that the movement was the wind blowing the curtain through an open window. From the vent pipes on the roof and just above the window, they figured it to be the kitchen.

"There are several trees for cover until we get close to the house," said Wayne.

"We can all approach staying behind the line of sight of them."

"Why don't we just wait here for a while and see if anyone comes out?" piped Perra.

"Right now we're sitting ducks," Dane replied. "Anyone with a high-powered rifle could pick us off from that ridge," he said as he pointed to his left. "The sooner we get to that house, the safer I'll feel. Also, if people are there, they will probably be getting up soon. If they're not already up."

They split up again and headed for the house. They slowly zigzagged from tree to tree until they came to open grasslands. Instead of stopping, they lined up with a tree and the house, then followed a straight line in. As they all reached their target cover, they gave a thumbs up. Dane was on the left side with Wayne in the center. Dane was going to head to the pump house while Wayne headed for a tree between the pump house and the shed, where Perra would go.

Wayne hated the fact that he was putting Perra in possible danger. She looked way out of her element holding her .22 semi automatic rifle. He knew that Dane was right about three weapons being available if needed.

Dane was in his element here. He had spent twenty years in the Army. His knowledge of survival and use of weapons were invaluable. His guidance kept them aware of their surroundings and of the possible hiding places for an ambush.

Wayne lifted up his binoculars, so he could see if anyone were inside. At the same time that he could make out a person in the kitchen window, chunks of bark flew apart not four inches from his face. Before he could react, he heard the crack of a small-caliber weapon. He spun around to hide behind the narrow tree. He had to get out of there, since the tree was only about six inches in diameter.

Dane laid down cover fire as Wayne bolted to the shed, where Perra stood in shock. By the time he reached the shed, blood had trickled down his left cheek.

Perra was only frozen for a second, then took her pack off and reached for her first-aid kit. She quickly cleaned then put a band aid on the small cut.

"Step out again," they heard. "I won't miss this time."

"We're not here to fight you. We are only looking for other people," yelled Wayne.

"You have a lot of nerve coming back here."

"We haven't been here before," added Dane. "We are your neighbors from a few miles from here. My brother and his wife are here too. We mean you no harm."

"There's nobody living within five miles of here. I checked."

"We live in an underground shelter. You wouldn't have seen us," said Dane from behind the pump house.

"You mean the small shelter south of here? It's too small. You're lying, go away or I will shoot you."

Suddenly Perra stepped out from the shed with her hands to her side. "My name is Perra, and what he said is true. We live close to the small shelter. Please, my husband is bleeding. We only want to see if others are still alive," she pleaded.

Wayne almost leaped out to get his wife when she suddenly stepped out. Again she surprised him with her courage, *or craziness*, he thought, but the ploy seemed to work.

"All right, but leave your guns where I can see them. I thought you were the two guys that came last year. I know *now* that you aren't, because I shot one of them in the leg. He would still be limping by now.

They reluctantly left their weapons leaning against the front of the shed and came closer. Dane still had his Glock 9mm in his shoulder holster, safely hidden under his coat. The only drawback was that his coat was still zipped up.

As they came closer to the window, they could see a dark haired young woman, maybe in her mid twenties.

"What's the zip code here?" She asked.

"I don't know. We never received mail here before. I had the shelter built so we could hide and never put in a mail box."

She seemed to ponder that for a few seconds as the three looked down her rifle barrel.

"Fair enough, so who was the owner of the land that you purchased?"

"We purchased it through Thatcher Ranch," said Wayne. "We bought 45 acres about four years ago."

"What is the nearest town?" She asked.

"That would be Colorado City."

"Wait there," she said. The rifle barrel and her face disappeared.

Several seconds later she came out of the house with her rifle lowered, but ready. She was thin but solidly built. They could tell that she had spent most of her life on a ranch. Her cowboy boots were well worn and scuffed up.

"So what happened with the two guys you mentioned earlier," Dane asked.

"They caught us by surprise. They were waiting in the house when we got back from hunting. They killed my husband and almost raped me. Lucky for me I keep a loaded Smith and Wesson under my pillow. It was very unlucky for them. I tried to shoot that bastards dick off, but I missed. I think I blew his knee cap off though. The other one doesn't have part of his left ear. Last I saw them they were heading north as fast as they could go."

Under the sunlight, they could clearly see some strands of grey hair. Her deep blue eyes were strong and sincere. Now that they could see her better, they could tell that she was in her late thirties, maybe early forties.

"I've been waiting for those bastards to come back for a long time now. When I saw you coming here kind of sneaky like, I figured it was *them* coming back for a second try. I didn't see you at all," she said as she pointed her nose at Perra.

Perra beamed proudly at her husband. She stepped forward and held out her hand.

"I'm so happy to meet you. It's wonderful to see another woman after so long."

The lady did not hesitate and stepped forward with her own hand.

"You can call me Connie."

Introductions went around, then she invited them in. The place was not too dark inside. Enough light came in from a skylight and a few windows to see well. It was then that they could see bars and on the windows, and sandbags under them. There were several rifles leaning in various areas of the house.

"I saw the old truck outside and *thought* somebody was still around," confided Dane. "At first I couldn't figure out why, and then all of a sudden it came to me."

"How did you know by looking at my truck," Connie asked.

"There were no weeds around the tires. If it had not been driven, it would have had weeds growing all around it."

"Very observant," she said with a small smile. Did you also figure out why my truck is still running?"

"As a matter of fact, I have," he said with his own small smile. "Your truck is old enough that it didn't have any electronic components in it for the EMP's to fry. What year is that? A '72?"

"Close, it's a '71 Ford. It's got enough miles to have been to the moon and back. Of course, the engine's been replaced a few times."

"Have a seat, please, I don't have much to offer, but the water is cold and refreshing." Looking at Wayne, she said "I'm sorry I almost shot you. Is your cheek okay?"

"Yes, it's just a small cut. I'm glad you're not a very good shot," he said as he pulled his finger away to check for blood.

"Actually, I'm an excellent shot. In my haste to put a bullet between your eyes, the scope got bumped. I'm relieved that I missed though," she said as she pierced him with her bright blue eyes.

"You almost caught me outside getting water from the well."

"Are you alone here," Dane asked.

"Yes." She replied with a slightly guarded look. "I couldn't stop my son, Chris, from heading out to find his girlfriend. He had done that several times since the storms stopped. A few months ago I found his truck about five miles down the interstate. I haven't seen him since."

"Oh, I'm so sorry Connie," Perra said as she got up and hugged the taller woman.

The women went to fetch some water from the kitchen.

The two brothers removed their packs and laid out their snacks. As the two women came back in, Perra did the same, so they could all share a snack.

"You have honey?" Connie asked wide eyed.

"We stocked up on lots of stuff," said Perra a between bites.

"I've been living on mostly deer and elk. When I can get one, I cook it up and can it."

After a big bite, "Oh, this tastes so good! I am out of most of the other stuff I had, but I can trade some canned meat for honey, if you've got more," she said with biscuit crumbs on the side of her mouth.

"Do you have anything else to trade?" She asked. "I've got lots of meat, and I'm starting to get tired of it."

"I think we might be able to arrange something," said Wayne.

"I'm sorry to have to ask," said Dane, "but how did your husband die?"

"They jumped him after we came in from tending to the cattle," she said wiping her mouth. It was no easy feat for them to knock Tom out, since he had been a rancher all of his life, but they got in a lucky shot. When he was out, they came after me. They made me watch as they tied his hands behind his back, then beat him some more. When they were finished, they stabbed him in the back." Tears were in here eyes, but her voice was firm as she continued, "After that they drug me into the bedroom. The rest you already know."

The brothers looked at each other as they realized the connection between this place and the last.

"I buried him that night. I was going to follow them the next day, but my son had just come back from one of his trips. He pleaded with me to stay. The next time he left I headed north. They had two weeks on me, so I had a tough time tracking them. I tracked them to a place on the ridge where they killed everyone. I knew it was them because of the way the man died. The wife and daughter had been raped. I just closed the doors and left. I tried to track them some more, but all trace was gone."

"Yes, we found that family on the ridge and buried them," Wayne said. "I was silently hoping we would run into them," he said with a dangerous look in his eyes.

"You have lots of fire power here, how come they didn't take your weapons," Dane asked.

"We put in a gun safe after Chris shot off one of his little toes, so they were always locked up."

"Where did your son get the gas to drive around," Dane asked, changing the subject.

"Oh, we converted our trucks to propane years ago. We have a two-thousand gallon tank inside the large shed by the driveway. We also use it for cooking and heating."

They were all silent for a few moments, and then Dane asked bluntly, "Why don't you come and live with us?"

Wayne nodded his approval. His wife added, "Oh yes, it is much safer where we live, and it's not far from here. We could leave a note for your son if… I mean… when he returns."

They could plainly see the hesitancy on her face and in her body language.

"I... I don't know. This house has been my home for over twenty years." She sat with her head down. "My husband and I were married out by the Red Maple. I buried him in the same spot we traded vows. My…son…" she sobbed quietly.

Perra slid over a little and gave her a hug. Connie seemed to draw strength from the physical contact.

"What do you want?" She suddenly asked. What plans do you have?"

"We're just looking for other peaceful people, hopefully someone with a ham radio," Wayne said.

"I'll be back in a minute," Connie said. She stood up and went down the hall. They heard a door close. After a few minutes, she came back out looking somewhat composed.

"I know I should have moved away from here after my husband was killed, but with my son coming and going I had to stay. I've had nothing but trouble here, and I've been terribly lonely. When the storms hit, all of my cattle and horses disappeared, then my dog died few months later. I know; it sounds like a country song," she said with a sad smile.

"The safest place here is the root cellar, where I keep the canned food, but it's too small to stay in for very long. I guess what I'm saying is that I will come with you," she said with a smile full of heartache.

"I know where the house is if I need to come back, but I don't expect to see my son again," she said bravely.

They all took turns giving her a hug and welcoming them to the "family".

Dane seemed highly pleased.

"I'll leave a note for Chris if he ever shows up. Of course, I'll want to come back and check every so often," she said.

"So where the hell *is* your place," she asked as she wiped the moisture from her eyes. "I've been all over the hills and only found a small shelter with room enough for one. There was a small car hidden under a camouflage net beside it."

They all took turns explaining to her about the shelter and how well they had hidden it. Connie was dumbfounded when she found out that she had actually walked right over the top of it.

They decided to use the truck to haul the weapons and as much food, clothing and bedding as they could for the trip back. Following the road, it only took them ten minutes to reach the area where they needed to turn off. There was no road heading to the shelter.

A few places on the main road were grown over, but most of it was still in fairly decent shape. They drove between the short trees and stopped by the small shelter. The car beside it was covered with old leaves and camouflage netting. A large branch had broken off from an Aspen a year before and destroyed the engine.

They showed her the mechanism to get into the main shelter, but explained that they could not get in that way because the door swung inside, and they had it blocked. They then took her back outside and up to the fake rocks and showed her how they worked.

"Son of a bitch!" She exclaimed. I sat on that rock when I came through here. I felt something wasn't right when I was sitting there. I just couldn't put my finger on it at the time. I figured I was just being paranoid. Almost like someone was watching me," she said shaking her head.

"Come on in," said Dane as he started climbing down.

Connie was genuinely amazed at the set-up and how well it worked. It was much bigger than she realized. What she liked most was that you could run up one set of stairs, run across the shelter to the other side, and run down the other set.

Her "room" was between Dane and the married couple.

"This might take some time to get used to," she said after inspecting the place. "I'm so used to being out under the sky."

"It took us a while to get used to it, but it's not too bad. Since we've been getting outside the last week or so it does seem to get a little stuffy," said Wayne. "The good news is that we're on a mission and will be ranging out further and further every day," he added.

"Like I said before, there's nobody within five miles of here, except us," she added. "I've walked and driven a lot of these hills. I've even driven down the highway looking for my son. Everywhere I've looked has been empty."

Wayne and Dane just nodded as they digested the information.

CHAPTER 7
AN ADDITION

They helped Connie move her stuff in and get settled. They showed her how to pump the water and set up the solar heater.

"A hot shower?" She exclaimed. "Oh, I've missed that so much!" I've had warm baths, but it takes *so* long to heat the water, pour it in the bathtub, heat more and so on. I just can't believe how simple this set up is."

"It took us a while to get used to it, but it works fine, even though the water doesn't get very hot," said Perra.

"So where's the solar panel," Connie asked. "I didn't see one out there."

"I used a lot of smaller panels and put them in trees, then I painted them in camouflage colors to blend in better," Wayne said.

Connie simply nodded a few times, and then went back to organizing her things.

They made a few more trips to her ranch and soon had her settled. She grabbed the rest of her weapons, ammunition and personal belongings. She wrote a letter to her son, locked the place up and tried not to cry as they headed back to the shelter. Perra suggested that they all move back in as soon as they knew the area was safe. Connie was readily amenable, but Dane and Wayne were somewhat reluctant. After an in depth discussion, they finally agreed that it would be gratifying to live in a normal house again, even one without power. Wayne brought up the idea of using the solar power from the Marshall's house. It would take a few trips and a lot of work, but they could run a refrigerator, have a hot shower, and could have some lights at night, depending on how large the system was.

"I went in that house too," Connie said. "I thought the solar panels were a bit too big for the house. As I recall, it wasn't very big."

"What did you find in there?" Dane asked quickly.

"I hardly found anything useful. The food was all gone, of course, but it surprised me that there was running hot water. When the light in the pantry came on, it scared the hell out of me. I'd briefly thought of taking the shelves, so I could use them to board up some of my windows back at the ranch, but figured it would be too much of a hassle. Besides, I still have some boards left from the old barn that we tore down a few years ago," she added.

Her fair skin turned whiter as they told her of the bounty just a few yards away from where she had stood.

"Son of a bitch, I was that close to all that food?" She exclaimed. "You'll have to show me!"

They all laughed at the comical way she cursed. It certainly helped lighten everyone's mood. Wayne suddenly realized they had hardly laughed for the last several months. It felt refreshing and seemed to brighten everyone up.

At dinner that night they discussed their next place to visit. Although Connie had already been through most of the houses in the area, they decided to recheck them all. It was possible other people could have moved in since she went through them. Also, she could not remember seeing any large antennas sticking up from the roofs. She was not paying attention at the time. She had only been looking for the two slime bags that killed her husband.

They debated whether or not to use the truck. The propane in the large tank was almost half way gone, which was still a considerable amount, but once they ran out, there was no way to get more. There was also the fact that the truck was not very quiet when going over all of the bumps and dips in the dirt road. They soon decided that they would only use it for transporting essential items back to the shelter, or if they went further than three miles.

Connie was adamant about seeing the cache at the Marshall's, so they planned their next trip heading out that direction. They would stop and check on the solar panels and operating system, the hidden stash, and then head out to the next house another mile or so from there.

Perra felt excited about getting to see the stash, since she had only heard about it. She decided to grab some chocolate first, since she was a chocoholic and had not had any for over a year. Her mouth watered at the thought of eating some smooth, creamy chocolate again.

CHAPTER 8
A MUTT

They all rose early the next morning and ate a quick breakfast of rolled oats with cinnamon and honey. The women had prepared food for their trek the night before. Afterwards, they realized they could have just eaten what they wanted at the Marshall's place.

The guys came up from below with weapons and other gear while the women finished putting the food into a few back packs. Dane handed each of them a weapon before they started to climb the ladder.

They decided to split up into two groups. Dane and Connie were in the front as they headed south. This time the trip was a little faster than the first time. They found the game trail and were soon at their destination. After quietly surveying the house for a while, Dane approached the front of the house. The door was still open, just as they had seen it the week before. Connie went around back and came forward as Dane went through the living room to the kitchen.

Wayne and Perra waited for the "all clear" sign before

breaking cover. They quickly went into the house, hoping everything was still there.

"I don't think anybody's been here since we were here last," said Dane.

They showed the women the way into the pantry, the trick to entering the hidden shelter, then the stairs leading down. In order for them to get the full effect, they let the women go down first. Although they knew what to expect, they still gasped as they saw the bounty. Perra let out a little squeal as she ran to a box of chocolates, vacuum sealed in a plastic bag.

They all seemed to forget their circumstances as they huddled around Perra. She handed out a few pieces to each one of them as their mouths watered. The two women almost seemed to melt as they savored their sweets. The two men gobbled theirs as their eyes surveyed the area. Dane went several feet along one lane and turned left as Wayne went to the right.

"Here's the bathroom," said Dane. They could hear him peeing, and then heard the flush of a toilet, then water running.

"Shit, that water's hot!" They heard him exclaim.

Wayne was checking out a tumbled mess of unopened electronic boxes. They were stacked haphazardly, then fell over. He moved a few boxes aside and picked up two sets of walkie-talkies. He dug through the pile and came up with rechargeable batteries and chargers.

"Jackpot," he said as he held them up for others to see.

They all started looking through the shelter and took turns exclaiming about their discoveries. After about ten minutes, Dane realized that they were wasting time and announced that he was going up stairs to check on the solar system.

Wayne put the radios in his backpack and headed up after him. They quickly found the panels, inverter and batteries.

"Have you ever worked on one of these before," Dane asked.

"No, I haven't worked on anything this complex." Wayne studied the system for several seconds. "I know that this inverter is a good one. I read something about them a few years ago. The better the inverter the better the sine wave is. It has something to do with the power output. If we draw this layout on paper, I think we can put it back together at Connie's place."

"There are plenty of spare wire spools, tools and other items we can use down stairs."

"Okay." Wayne said with emphasis.

"We'd better get going, before the ladies gorge themselves on chocolate," said Dane.

Wayne laughed as he said, "We won't be able to keep up with them after all that sugar hits their system."

Dane had an image of the girls with chocolate smeared around their mouths while sucking the melted chocolate off their fingers. He let out a quick laugh, and then headed back through the kitchen and into the hidden shelter.

Wayne quickly opened the walkie-talkies, batteries and chargers and plugged them in to charge. He figured they could stop back by on the way back and pick them up. Two-way radios would be invaluable in their search for other people. The range was not far, but they were good enough to keep them all better informed whatever the situation. It would also allow them to keep further apart, and ensure them more protection. They decided that when they were in pairs, they would only use one set and save the batteries of the other set.

"Why do you think he bought two sets of radios," Perra asked.

"Probably in case one set wore out or got broke. These are nice, but not real good for these hills," said Dane as he looked one over.

"This will change our tactics quite a bit, but we can still go silent if we see anything. We should probably come up with a signal or code word if we need to shut the radios off. I guess we could just scratch on the microphone before we shut it off. It may be the quietest way to signal when we are out of sight of each other."

"Okay, what do you say we close this up and go check out the next house," Wayne asked.

They closed up the shelter and put the boards back, and then closed the door to the pantry. They headed out the back of the house and took up the same formation they had before, with Dane and Connie in the front.

The game trail they came in on continued south along the base of the ridge, sometimes heading off in different directions. The trail faded away at a small creek that came out of the ridge, so they kept going south until they found a twisting dirt road. They had to track back and forth until they found the house. It was an A-frame house with two stories. It looked fairly new. The separated garage stood with gaping doors. There were no cars inside.

The evergreen trees were fairly thick in this part of the hills. The tallest was not much over twenty-five feet. The house, painted to fit in with the background, was just about as tall.

As Dane and Connie approached, they fanned out to either side of the front of the house. It was evident that nobody had been there for a long time. A thin Poplar tree had fallen against one side of the angled roof. The screen door was hanging by one hinge, and the front door appeared to be closed. They could see inside, but there was not much to see. They went around back to check on the back door, which they found unlocked. Connie accidentally kicked a dirty, chewed up, dog bowl that made them both jump. They just looked at each other for a second then Connie mouthed "sorry". Dane flashed a quick smiled and turned to the door. The hinges creaked as Dane slowly opened it. He paused for a minute straining to hear. There was no sound coming from inside, so they continued into the house.

The air seemed very stuffy and had a strange smell they could not place. They continued into the living room and to the stairs leading to the second floor. Dane led the way upstairs with his rifle up and ready. Connie stayed at the bottom with her rifle up, as well.

Dane slowly went up the stairs but froze when a step creaked under his weight. Heart pounding, he ran up the last few steps quickly. He crouched on the last two steps when he got near the top. He swung his rifle side to side as he stood up and went to the doorway of a small bathroom. As he turned, he discovered the strange smell. The bodies of a young man and woman lay on the bed together, dressed in nice clothes. The man was on his back while the lady was on her side with her head on his chest. She had in her hand an envelope. Dane did not need to take it and read it to know what had happened.

Connie could see him from the bottom of the stairs, and knew he found something terrible. As Dane came down the stairs, she went to the front door and waved to the other two.

Wayne went up to see and took the note back down stairs. The young couple had just been married and been on their honey moon when society crumbled. The young woman's father's antique car had been stolen, and left them stranded. After their food was gone, they took some poison and lay down together, for the last time.

Even though Perra did not go up the stairs, she started to cry. Connie took her out on the front porch, cleaned off a chair and had her sit down.

As the guys looked through the house, they heard a soft growl mixed in with a whine. They immediately brought their weapons up and swivelled to the sound. With Dane in front, they followed the sound out the back door and a few yards into the trees.

At first they thought it was a small bear then discovered it was a medium sized dog. It was extremely thin and seemed to have a hard time breathing. It started to whine, and lay down with its tail between its legs. Wayne slowly approached the mangy thing, trying to figure out why it was acting so strangely. The dog growled then whined again.

Wayne took off his pack slowly and pulled out some dried beef jerky they found at the Marshall's. The dogs' head jerked up at the smell. It was evidently scared, and nearly dead from malnutrition. As Wayne threw the dog a piece of the meat, he saw the problem. The nylon collar was cutting off the poor thing's wind pipe.

Wayne watched as the dog tried to swallow the piece of meat whole. It got caught in the dogs' throat until it coughed it back up. It tried again, this time chewing it better before swallowing. Wayne softly talked to it as he fed it a few smaller pieces then made it come closer for more food. After a few minutes, the dog allowed him to pet its head.

He could see the dog was male, and seemed to have had

the collar put on when it was mostly grown. The hair was rubbed off under the collar.

Moving slowly, he unbelted the collar. The dog whined as he removed it, taking off a little skin. The poor thing peed a little but was hesitantly wagging his tail.

"That's a good boy," he said as he patted his head.

"You want some more food, don't you?"

The dog weakly looked up with his big brown eyes and shook his tail some more.

Dane had been watching with mild disgust on his face. "We don't need a dog following us around. We should just kill it and finish up here."

Wayne quickly stood up and turned to face his brother, his face clouded.

"NO! I will *not* kill this dog," he said vehemently.

"Do you know what type of dog this is?" he asked his older brother.

"No, and I don't care. Where would we keep it? What would we even feed the damn thing? It's almost dead anyway."

Dane turned to walk away, but his brother's voice stopped him.

"This is a hunting dog, Dane. If you want to make sure an area is clear, this dog will let us know. I'm not sure if he's trained, but he's still young enough to make a good tracker. He'll even let us know if someone else is sneaking around in the trees. I'm bringing him back. We can use the front entryway if we need to, but I'm *not* leaving him behind."

Dane stood there with his back to his brother. After a pregnant pause he muttered, "Fine," and walked back into the house.

A few seconds later the women came around the side of

the house. They spotted the dog and hurried over to Wayne's side.

"Where did you find him?" Connie asked.

Perra was next to the dog petting him and crooning in her native language.

"Ok ka lang?" She said, asking him if he were okay. "Oh, poor puppy," she continued in English.

The dog seemed to perk up a lot in the last few minutes and was sitting up and loving the attention. His eyes were on Perra as she continued her baby talk. His tail seemed to speed up considerably too.

"We heard him when we were inside. We came out, and he was right here. That's got to be his dog dish by the back door that I almost tripped over."

"Once he puts on some weight, this will be a fine dog," announced Connie. "He's been malnourished for a long time, but he'll be okay after a couple of good baths and lots of good meals. I have just the stuff for his neck back at the ranch," she added.

"Oh, I'm so glad to hear that," said Perra. "When he is better, can we eat him?" She asked with a straight face.

Connie drew back in horror. "Oh...of course not," she said with her voice dripping disgust.

"Why not," Wayne asked, playing along. "When he packs on some muscle, this guy will feed us for a week, at least."

Connie took turns just staring at her new friends. Finally, Wayne could not keep his face straight any longer, and burst out laughing. Perra just smiled a Cheshire grin.

"Oh! You two! I thought you were serious," Connie said as she lightly punched Wayne in the shoulder. "That was a good one," she added.

"I think we have a few more things to give this dog for some strength to get back to the shelter. He *is* coming back with us, right," Perra asked.

"This dog is in no shape to be walking." Connie, evidently the animal expert, replied. "I don't think he would have lasted more than few days if we hadn't come along. We can take turns carrying him. If he wants to walk, we will let him, but he'll probably slow us down."

"Well, we're not in any hurry. Let's take turns, but we still need to keep an eye out," Wayne said. Dane had already gone back into the house.

They completed a search of the house and garage. Nothing of use remained except a set of knitting needles and the dog bowl. Wayne thought, "What the heck," and grabbed both.

Using a board he found in the garage, they scraped enough dirt aside in which to lay the dead couple. They simply wrapped them in the blankets they died on, carried them down to the grave site, and covered them up. Perra insisted on putting the board into the ground with a few words scratched into it.

They headed back soon afterward The girls walked behind the men, taking turns carrying the dog. They stopped to rest at the Marshall's place. Dane and Wayne went downstairs to get the walkie-talkies. They put in the batteries, did a signal test, then clipped them to their belts. Then they put an extra radio in both of their packs. They had to leave the chargers there, since there was no other place to use them. Ideally, they needed to charge them for several hours, but they did not want to wait three more hours for them to be ready.

They left the house and headed back to their home. This time the dog felt good enough to walk, albeit slowly. Dane was still not sure they needed the dog, but slightly warmed to him when he came over and looked up at him as they were walking.

"So you want to be my friend too, huh?" He asked. "You sure are a pathetic mutt". He reached down and briefly scratched his head.

When they reached the shelter, Wayne went in through one of the hidden entrances. He then went down and moved the large block, then opened the front entry way. The dog padded into the shelter as if he knew the place. Perra pulled out some worn out blankets and put them in a corner, where the dog sniffed for a moment, then turned around a few times, lay down, and promptly went to sleep.

"So what are we going to call him?" Perra asked later that night. They discussed different names for a while then decided on Lucky. The name fit his circumstances perfectly.

They stayed home for a few days after that, periodically testing the range of the radios. Wayne ran some wire from a tree above the shelter inside where they could hook it to the antenna of the radio. It was a little better than being outside with it, but not much.

As soon as Lucky gained some weight, Connie started training him. She had trained several of her previous dogs and knew how to get them to track game, point and retrieve. Wayne gave her some small scraps of rabbit hide to use in teaching him how to track. She also taught him basic obedience skills. The dog was quick to learn and loved to play after his lessons. Very few times did they have to clean up his messes inside the shelter.

CHAPTER 9
NO REVENGE

As they began to range further and further from the shelter, Dane and Connie got closer and closer. Sometimes, to Wayne's discomfort, they would take the dog and disappear for a few hours. After several trips, they came back hand in hand.

Soon the mornings came earlier, and the days warmed pleasantly. Before long August rolled around.

Their trips took longer and longer to complete, and they all toned up and felt much better. They occasionally stopped by the Marshall's place and grabbed a few needed items but left the majority of the supplies there.

By the end of summer they visited almost all of the houses in the area. There was still no sign of anybody else, and certainly no working ham radio.

They started to use the truck when their walks started taking all day. One morning they headed up the road on top of the ridge. Dane was inside the cab with Connie. Wayne, Perra, and Lucky were in the back. They went several miles when Perra barely spotted another house that they missed before. The road was completely over grown and was hardly visible through the trees, grass and shrubs.

Dane cautiously drove up to the house and parked out front. As soon as they stopped, Lucky jumped out and headed into the trees near by. Connie knew he was on to something, but was not sure why he was acting so strange.

They all jumped out of the truck together. They had their weapons ready as they headed into the trees. A short way into them the dog stood in a pointing posture. He was pointing at a brown mound on the ground about twenty feet ahead.

Dane and Wayne slowly went ahead with their weapons pointed forward.

"Lucky! Come!" Connie said tersely.

He reluctantly came back to her and heeled.

The bear had been dead for a while, and the same went for the two men that lay near by. By the looks of it, they had been dead for maybe three months.

One of the men was partially hidden underneath the bear. A compound bow with the string broken lay nearby.

"That's a weird way to end up," Dane said as he pointed to the man under the bear.

As the other two women came over, they all saw what looked like a spear in the chest of the bear.

Dane bent down where a pistol lay nearby. He opened the revolver and saw that the only two rounds inside had been fired. "Empty," he said as he showed the others.

Connie stiffened as she looked closer at one of the dead men.

"It looks like I won't get my revenge after all," she said quietly.

"Are those the men that killed your husband," Dane asked just as quietly.

"I recognize the gun shot wound to this guys knee cap," she said pointing.

"I'm sure these are the guys that came after me." Wayne added. "I recognize that coat."

"It looks like the bear made a snack out of his leg." Connie said as she bent over and looked at the teeth marks on his thigh bone." She quickly plugged her nose as the wind shifted.

Dane reached over pulled on the broken shaft that was sticking in the chest of the bear. It came out fairly easily, but the end was not sharp. He puzzled that over for a second, then reached in the hole and pulled out a large kitchen knife.

In piecing the puzzle together, they figured that the bear caught one guy and started eating. The other guy came by to help his friend. The bear probably lunged at him, got stuck by the spear, and broke the shaft as it fell on the second man. The bear died with its teeth in the guy's neck.

"Served them right," Connie said bitterly. "Let's leave them where they are, they aren't good enough to bury." She turned and walked away with Lucky at her side.

As they left the area, Dane threw the knife on the ground near the bear. This was one time he did not want to keep a knife.

They went back by the truck and up to the house. They had relaxed their approach to the houses these days. Week after week they found the same thing. The houses were either abandoned, looted, or had dead bodies in various places. This house was unusual. The place seemed cleaner than most. There was evidence that someone lived there for quite a while after the power went out. There were kerosene lanterns around the house. The candles looked as if they were used after the kerosene ran out. A garden in the back was full of weeds and looked as if it sprouted from last years unpicked crops.

Off to one side, with an awe-inspiring view of a small valley, they found two graves. They were both slightly overgrown with weeds and grass. Just to one side they found the remains of what looked like a man. A rusted pistol was still in his skeletal grip.

A few of them just sighed, went back to the truck and grabbed some shovels, then went back to add another mound to the group.

There was little that they needed from the house. The women found some good clothes from the bedrooms. They were laundered and neatly folded in dressers or hung on hangers in the closets.

They only took what they would use, then closed the place and left.

CHAPTER 10
RETURN FROM THE DEAD

Connie was unusually quiet for the rest of the day. The next day, early in the morning, she took Lucky and drove away for a while. Dane was almost fit to be tied when he found out she went off by herself.

"She isn't by herself." Perra said. "She has Lucky with her. Just give her a little time to process her feelings. Don't you dare say anything about her leaving you behind. This is about her, not you."

Dane merely stared at her for a few seconds then seemed to deflate.

"You're right, Perra, thanks." He thought for a few seconds then added, "At the very least, she should have taken a radio with her."

"She did," said Wayne walking up to them. "She also took her hunting rifle."

A half hour later the truck came flying up through the trees. Someone was in the truck with Connie. The truck came to a sliding halt as she jumped out. Lucky jumped out the back of the truck and followed her to the passenger side.

Dane rushed out of the small shelter, where he had been sitting and trying to make some arrowheads.

"Connie, are you alright? Who is that in the truck?" He said as he came around to the passenger side.

"This is my dad, Frank," she said with teary eyes.

The old man looked awful. His skin had red blotches, and patches of his hair had fallen out. His sunken eyes looked rheumy.

"He's been at the ranch for a few days. If I had not left some food there for Chris, he probably would have been dead by now. We went right by the place and didn't even know he was there!" She said with passion.

They lifted out the barely conscious man. He seemed mostly skin and bones.

"Where did he come from?"

He has a farm northeast of Denver. In order to get here, he must have come through at least two radiation zones." She said tearfully.

Wayne and Perra heard the ruckus and came out to see what was going on. Nowadays they usually kept the front access way into the shelter open. They were careful to make sure they secured it each time they left.

They carried Connie's father into the shelter and laid him on the bed she and Dane shared. He seemed so light and frail. In the condition he was in, it was a wonder that he made it this far.

Wayne turned to his wife. "Perra, can you please get the Potassium Iodide tablets from the large First-aid kit?" He turned back to Connie. "We have some pills that will help with the radiation, but I'm not sure how many RADS he's had, or for how long. Were you able to talk to him?"

"He's said very little. He mumbled something about his little pumpkin, which is what he used to call me when I was a little girl."

"We need to get him out of these clothes and into the shower. Any radiation we can get off of him will help."

They quickly stripped him to his underwear and carried him into the shower. Hot water was ready since Perra had already heated the water for her shower. Even though it was summer, the ground water was still very cold and did not want to put him through any more shock.

Once they used up all of the hot water, they wrapped him in a blanket and put him on the middle bed. It was unused now that Connie moved over to Danes bed.

Wayne pulled out a precious bag of saline solution, inserted a needle into a vein on Frank's right arm then hung it from the line that held the blanket they used for privacy.

Connie was wringing her hands while Wayne put some tape across the needle and then adjusted the flow.

We need to flush his system, but all we have are five of the saline solution bags. Hopefully he will wake up and be able to talk to us soon," he said doubtfully.

"There were a few hospitals in Pueblo. If he needs more I will go get some," Dane said sincerely.

"Wouldn't it be radioactive?" Perra asked.

"Not necessarily," Dane said. "Those hospitals are big, and the prevailing wind probably took most of the radiation east, or south east from there. The bigger the building, the more protection you have from radiation. Besides, most of the targets were out east. I'd bet money there are still plenty of bags left there."

"I still can't believe he made it all this way," Wayne said as he stood there looking down at the frail old man. The sheer determination of the man was awe inspiring. The drive to see his daughter before he died was astounding.

"How far do you think he came?" Perra asked her husband.

"By highway it's about a hundred and seventy miles. You have to know my Dad. He's always been a tough one. Ever since Mom died, he's run the farm mostly by himself. I'm surprised it took him this long to get here. I thought that since he did not show up after the first few months that he had died along with everybody else," she said guiltily.

Wayne went to get the wind up dosimeter while the other three stayed by Frank. He gave the handle about twenty turns, then turned it on and held it over Frank's chest. Two to three clicks came out each second, depending on where he held it. Wayne was genuinely surprised that it was not more.

"What the hell?" He asked. "If he came through the contaminated areas along I-25, then he should be lighting this thing up a lot more than this."

Turning to Connie he asked, "How did he get to your place?"

Without looking up she said, "He rode in on a bike. The back tire was flat. He had a backpack and his hunting rifle. He never goes anywhere without his rifle."

"Pumpkin, that you?" Her Dad suddenly asked.

Connie knelt down suddenly and grabbed his left hand.

"Yes Dad, it's me."

"I wasn't sure if you were still alive," he said with more vigor than they all thought possible.

"I had to come down and see for myself. Where are we? This isn't your ranch. Where are Tom and Chris?"

"Shhh…you should rest for a little while," she said.

Franks blue eyes took on a glinting hardness.

"Don't you shush me young lady." Suddenly he sat up and looked down at the blanket.

"Where in heavens name are my clothes?" He said indignantly.

"We had to take them off because of the radiation."

"Radiation? Bah! I drove around most of it. I went west through Loveland Pass, then worked my way down south. I came out through Canon City. There are still people back in the mountains, by the way. Not too friendly, but I honestly can't blame them. Once I got through Canon City someone took a shot at me and clipped the line on the propane tank. I was able to patch it up a little, but I finally ran out just west of Pueblo. I managed to find a place to hole up for the night. The next morning I found a mountain bike and rode it down here. I was so worn out by the time I got here that I slept for most of a day. I think I ate something bad because I ended up with a really bad stomachache and fever. The only thing I could take were some allergy pills, which kicked my ass and made me extremely sleepy. Now I wake up nearly naked surrounded by you and some strangers.

"If you don't have radiation sickness, why are your hair and skin like that," Wayne asked.

"Ever heard of scurvy?" He said as he warily eyed the stranger.

Wayne pondered for a few seconds then said, "Yes, it's something you get when you are vitamin deficient, a lack of fresh fruit."

"Bingo, boy. I ran out of dried and canned fruit a while back. The apple trees back at my ranch aren't ready to …"

"Dad, you really need to rest. You look worn out."

"That's because I *am* worn out, young lady. I just rode a mountain bike 35 miles, and about ten of that was on a flat tire, *and* my ass is sore." His eyes took in his surroundings, then the people standing around his bed.

"Where's Tom and Chris?" He asked again in a firmer voice.

Connie sat on the side of the bed and told him everything since the collapse. Her father took it in and simply nodded from time to time. The other three drifted off, so the father and daughter could catch up on current events.

A half hour later Connie came upstairs, where Perra was making lunch.

"He's sleeping now. Damned stubborn old man," she said looking down the stairs.

"A man his age shouldn't have even tried getting here, much less traveling alone, *and* on a bicycle," said Wayne.

"My dad is too stubborn to admit he can't do something. Even in his late sixties he was doing almost everything on the farm. I still feel as if this is a dream. I went back to the ranch so I could process my feelings. When I drove up to the house, I saw a bike leaning against the house and, at first, thought Chris was back. When I went in expecting to find him, I found Dad on the couch. This is all too crazy," she said shaking her head.

Keeping Frank in bed long enough to recover from scurvy was more trouble than any of them expected. He was extremely weak, but managed a string of profanities when they almost forced him to stay in bed. He only had enough energy to curse for a few minutes then had to rest. He also complained about the red splotches under his skin. Wayne looked up scurvy in his survival book and found out that the red splotches were pooled blood. Rather than let them pop open and possibly fester, they poked them with a sewing needle that Connie sanitized in rubbing alcohol. At least he did not cuss too much when he let them do it.

The vitamin C tablets they had stored were just passed the expiration date, but ended up serving their purpose. Within a week, the once feeble old man was up and getting around fairly well.

CHAPTER 11
REMINISCING

During the waning hot fall days, they gathered what fruits the trees produced and canned them. They foraged for any seeds that were edible and were able to find an overgrown field of wheat. It was wild, but they were able to gather plenty of seeds, even though it was hard work for people that had never collected it before. Frank was the most help when it came to knowledge of how to gather the stalks and separate the grain. His father used to do it the hard way when he was a kid working on *his* fathers' farm. He regaled them with stories of his youth.

"Pop almost died before I was born," he said with his usual blunt statements.

"The land dried up during the great depression, and he had to abandon the farm with his parents. Gramps, grandma, and Pop sold what little they could on the farm and headed out to Colorado." He grabbed another handful of wheat stalks and started whacking them on the bed sheet they got from the house nearby. "There was little work on the way, but work was work, even if it only paid for a meal each. On one long stretch of road, the truck broke down. Now, gramps was a wonder with all things mechanical, but just wasn't able to fix broken metal." He eyed the empty wheat stalks with a critical eye, tossed them aside and grabbed another batch. "Pop was 17 at the time. Gramps gave him the last of the money and had him walk about 15 or 20 miles back to the last town. When he got there, he bought the part, a sandwich, and a few gallons of ethanol and headed back out to the truck. About three quarters of the way back the sun is almost touching the horizon and Pop is tired and hungry. He stopped to rest for a minute on the side of the road, then picked up the gasoline and started walking again."

The others by now took a break and grabbed a cold drink of water. Dane had just finished unloading a large bunch of wheat stalks and was leaning on the pitchfork. Connie gave him a patient smile as she handed him the canteen. Wayne and Perra were tossing the grain into the air with another sheet and letting the wind take away all of the excess matter. They put down their sheet as they handed the canteen around.

Oblivious to the others, Frank continued his task. "Right on the side of the road was a large rattle snake. It had been basking in the sun, not twenty feet from where Pop stopped for a rest. Now, mind you, Pop was tired and hungry and was already thin from only one meal a day for quite some time. By the time he got to the snake, it had coiled up and was ready to strike," he said vigorously. "He spotted the snake just before he stepped on it. Instead of stepping on it he instinctively jumped to the side. Now, he was already off balance from the step that he did not take so when he jumped it was a wild flinging of his body to get away from the snake. Lucky for him the bite hit his leather boot and did not penetrate, but on the downside, he landed with the gasoline near his head. The top came off and splashed right into his eyes! Now he is blind, hungry, tired and almost just got killed by a rattle snake."

Frank stopped and noticed that everyone was hanging on his words like laundry on a clothes' line. He took a swig of the offered water and continued.

"You'd think most young men would break at that point. Do you know what he did?" He asked no one in particular. "He walked away from the snake several yards, took down his pants, and peed into his own eyes! Oh, he was a hootin' and a hollerin' from the gas, but when the pee cleared out some of it, he just hiked up his pants, grabbed the gas can and continued walking.

So here he is, alone on a deserted road, has gas and pee in his eyes, is hungry, tired and half blind when he hears what at first sounds as if a badly tuned car coming his way. He starts waving his arms trying to get the car to stop. Very quickly the sound gets louder and louder, and it scares him. He can't see what's coming so he starts running down the road away from it. Just as the airplane lands on the road, he jumps to the side and scrapes his shoulder."

Frank stops and takes another long pull from the almost empty canteen. Wiping the water from his chin with the back of this hand, he continued his story. "The plane coasts down the road, turns around, and comes back to Pop laying on the side of the road with gas and pee in his eyes, skinny as a worm, hungry, tired, and with a scraped up shoulder. By now the sun is halfway down on the horizon, but there was enough light for the pilot to see him when he almost landed on him."

"This tall, thin guy shuts down the engine, jumps out of

the plane and helps Pop up. He's bewildered to see this kid out in the middle of nowhere, smelling like gas and pee, with a scraped up shoulder, and lying on the side of the road, even though he knows he almost ran him over with the airplane. So the guy gives him some water and cleans him up a bit, asking him why he was out in the middle of nowhere, and how he got in his current condition. Then the tall guy opens the engine cowling as Pop explained how they had to leave the ranch, sell what they could, and how they had been working their way to Colorado. The guy couldn't seem to fix his problem with the plane, so he closed the cowling, had Pop get in the back and takes off again. So, here he is with a little less gas, has pee in his eyes, is tired, hungry, has a scratched up shoulder, and is riding in a plane he expects to crash at any moment."

The others by now are so engrossed with the story that they forgot about gathering and thrashing the wheat.

"A few minutes later the airplane suddenly dips. Pop thought he was going to die at that point. Luckily for him the pilot followed the road and landed next to Gramps' broke down pickup truck. I guess you could say that they were very surprised to see Pop jump out of the airplane smelling like gas and pee, with a scraped up shoulder, a half can of gas and the part for the truck. Well, after several minutes of landing, Pop has them all up to speed on what happened, including the scary ride in the airplane. Gramps then takes a look at the plane and has it fixed in no time."

"The guy is so happy that he gives Gramps all the money in his wallet, which was eighty-five dollars! Now that doesn't sound like much these days," he said forgetting that nobody used money anymore. "That much money was a house and car payment. So Gramps almost had a heart attack at seeing that much money, especially after being broke for so long. He refused to take that much, but the guy insisted on helping them get to Colorado, and wanted to make up for almost running over his one and only son and for helping me with the plane. The guy explains that he is taking his new airplane to an air show in Nevada and couldn't have got there without his help. He then gives Gramps a phone number to call, after he gets settled in Colorado, and leave an address so he can come out and visit."

By now they are all starting to get hungry, so they packed up the truck and headed back to the shelter. Frank is coming to his favorite part now and can't seem to hold it in any longer as he continues. "Gramps shakes his hand and realizes that he did not get the guy's name. So he asks, and as the guy in climbing back in his plane he says Howard, Howard Hughes. He fires up the plane, gives a little wave and off he goes. Now, you might think that's the end of the story," he says through the sliding window in the back of the truck so they can all hear. "They told a few people about it, but hardly anybody knew much of him. They pretty much forgot about the guy until Grandma came across the guy's name on the piece of paper and rang the number. They were not able to talk to Howard, but the lady seemed to be waiting for their call and took their address. They did not hear anything from him, and soon forgot about it. A few months later a guy came to the door asking if they were the ones that helped a guy fix his airplane several months before. Gramps said they were the ones, so the guy opens a brief case and pulls out a deed of trust for six hundred and forty acres. A note attached to it said, "Thanks for the help, your grateful friend, Howard."

Connie was shocked. She had never heard the story

before. She had only known that the land was given to them by someone really rich way before her birth. Everyone traded shocked looks as Frank sat in the back of the truck looking smug.

"Why didn't you tell me that before?" His daughter asked.

"I'd forgotten all about it until I remembered thrashing wheat with Pop back on the farm. I'd almost stepped on a rattler, and he told me the story. Of course, Pop was much more animated about it when he told me the story than I am."

Dane drove up the mild incline leading to the shelter as Frank finished up the story. They unloaded their gear and the twenty or so pounds of grain. They would dry it out for several days before running it through the hand grinder Wayne bought at a yard sale many years before. The fresh flour would be stored, and the old stock used up.

They went back day after day to harvest the wheat. It passed the time and soon the trees began to show some fall colors.

The last day of their harvest Connie realized something.

"Listen…" she said suddenly. "I had not realized this before, but there are birds singing." They all stopped to listen, and sure enough, they could hear many birds from a distance. None of them had seen more than a few birds all summer long. What they heard had to be hundreds. Suddenly they could see them swarm the field and land, busily chirping, scratching, and pecking at the feast before them.

They all just stood dumbfounded at the sudden appearance of the birds. They looked to be Swallows.

"Looks like nature is bouncing back after we messed

things up," Connie said. "I've been seeing more tracks and spore lately. If we're not careful, we're going to be overrun with deer, elk, fox, coyotes, rabbits and squirrels."

Lucky had been lying by the truck when the birds landed. He had probably never seen very many birds before. When they landed, he quickly scampered under the truck, only to peer out from behind a tire. Soon curiosity got the better of him as his predatory instinct came out. He looked at Connie then made a mad dash toward the closest of the birds. As they took off together, he turned right around and made another mad dash right back under the truck. This time with his tail tucked between his legs. They all started laughing, and even more so when they saw his nose poking out from under the truck again. "You big baby," Connie said as she laughed harder.

"Wouldn't it be nice to see large herds of deer and elk out grazing in the grasslands?" Wayne asked. The only time he had ever seen large herds of elk was when they were either raised on a farm, or when there was a government feeding program. He had seen small groups of deer, but nothing like the elk of years ago.

CHAPTER 12
THE TANK

That night after dinner, Wayne asked the group,"What does everyone think about heading south on the highway? I'd like to see if we can find anyone in Colorado City. We can put up some side walls on the back of the truck for protection if anyone takes a shot at us. By now, I just can't see there being many hostile people left."

"I've been down there looking for Chris, and I didn't see anyone," said Connie.

"How far did you go? Did you go passed San Isabel Lake? I know there were lots of houses near the reservoir. I also remember seeing the houses tucked up in the mountains years ago, and thought they would be an excellent place to hide out in case of an emergency."

"No, I never went further than the schools. I never thought Chris would go that far. I guess it's worth a look. I'm game, and no, I don't mind if you build side walls on my truck," she said with a sly smile aimed at Wayne.

"I've been thinking about it too," said Dane. Looking

pointedly at Frank he said, "You said there were still people back in the mountains, and that they weren't too friendly. Can you tell us any more about them?"

"Well, that was up north a bit. There weren't many of them. The ones I had a run in with were south-west of Denver and on the western side of the mountains. I was tired, so I looked for a nice bed to stay in," he said, going into his story telling mode.

"My energy was pretty low because of the scurvy. I found a ranch house set back off the main road and thought it was empty. There were no cars, trucks, lights, or even smoke from the chimney. So I pulled up to the house, shut the truck off and went up to the door. I knocked, but nobody answered, so I let myself in. It was too dark to see much, so I felt around and found a couch. I fell asleep fairly quickly and slept soundly until around daybreak. I was dead asleep until I hear two clicks. They were the type of clicks that come from a double-barrel shotgun getting ready to unload. I opened my eyes and saw a nasty lookin' fellow with the rifle. Next to him was a mangy-looking woman if I've ever seen one. Now, I don't go anywhere without my rifle, and that night was no exception. I'd pulled the afghan on the back of the sofa over me. The last thing I wanted was to be shot, much less having to shoot someone else, especially when I was trespassing kind of accidental like. So as soon as I open my eyes and see this shotgun pointed at my family jewels, I go into a fake coughing fit that would make Marlon Brando proud. They see the red spots on my face and my general condition and think I have something contagious. The guy with the shotgun turns white as a ghost and the woman steps back a few steps. Then, to my amazement, he says, "Lets get outta here Martha, this place ain't gonna be fit to live in now that it's contaminated."

"I laid there until they were out of sight, got up and got behind the couch with my rifle ready and waited to see if they were coming back. I heard some sounds coming from the kitchen, and then heard the back door slam. About five minutes later I crept through the living room, through the kitchen and peeked out the back door. They were saddling up a couple horses. One of them had a buggy attached to it with supplies. I figured that they didn't own the house and were squatters. I loaded up on whatever food and water they'd left, and headed out. The funny thing is," he said with a gleam in his eyes, "I passed them on the road heading south. You know what that ol' hag did to me? She gave me the middle finger as I passed them!" He guffawed and slapped his knee at the same time. "I just waved to them and smiled as big as a Cheshire cat when I passed. They're probably holed up at another abandoned farm house somewhere in the mountains."

"The only other time I saw anyone in the mountains was a few hours later, when I stopped to take a leak. Someone fired a shot. I don't know if they were aiming at me or just tried to scare me off. Could be they were hunting too, but either way I didn't waste time finding out. Other than that the person that shot my propane line on the truck was the last one I knew about."

"I figured there would be people still in Pueblo, but I didn't see any. I think the initial radioactive fallout from the Army Depot scared them enough that they moved out. Your Geiger counter seems to rule out much radiation left there now anyway."

"What about the roads," Dane asked.

"Well, most of the roads were still in reasonable shape. There were several places where the roads were either damaged or downright gone from all of the flooding.

"The old farm took a beating with all of that severe weather we had for so long, but I managed to keep dry until it pretty much stopped. I can tell you it got pretty boring just sitting there waiting month after month for the storms to stop. But, I digress. As I recall, the area you want to drive into was pretty rough country. I'll bet a bag full of two-bits that the reservoir is gone."

"You're probably right," Wayne said. "The mountains rise fairly high west of the reservoir. Any large amount of rain would quickly fill it up. As I recall it wasn't very big, and the spillway was rather small. The dam is made up of earth, with very little concrete. Now that I think about it, if it *is* gone, there was a road that went around it anyway."

"How far away is the dam, honey ko?" Perra said unexpectedly.

"As the crow flies it's several miles from here, but driving down the highway it's about twelve to fifteen miles. Not too far in your propane powered truck, though," he said, with a wink to Connie.

The rest of the night they hammered out the details of how to fit the truck with side walls thick enough to stop a bullet. They also decided it would be a good idea to get all four of the radios fully charged, just in case they had to split up.

After eating a nutritious breakfast, lunch was prepared and packed. They quickly went through the stored nails and screws and found what they needed. Next Dane brought out the old hand saws that his grandfather passed down. They were old, but still very usable. He grabbed two of them, a small handsaw, a few buckets, two hammers, two hand drills with wood and metal drill bits, a tape measure, a square, two Philips screw drivers, an assortment of nuts washers and bolts, and a pencil. As an after thought, he brought his old sheet rock square.

They came out through the false shelter to a cool, cloudy morning. The leaves had begun changing a few weeks before, and some stuck to the windshield of the truck.

In about five minutes, everything and everybody was loaded in the truck, plus a happy dog that seemed to know something special was happening.

Frank drove up the road under the direction of Dane. Wayne, Perra and Connie rode in the back with Lucky. He drove up to the Marshall's place and dropped off Dane, who went into the house and put all the radios on chargers, then closed up and returned to the truck. Next he drove to the A-frame house, again with directions from Dane.

As they pulled up to the garage, the dog jumped out and went running off, seeming to remember the place. Frank turned the truck around and backed it up to the garage. They all quickly unloaded the equipment in the back of the truck.

The two women grabbed the hammers and started prying off the vinyl siding. Dane and Wayne went inside to see if there were anything useful they could use. They found some old tools and a very dusty metal seven gallon gas container. It was empty, but still useful. The tools they set outside. There was a cabinet along the back wall with empty shelving. The guys took everything they could, even it if was nailed down.

"Ok guys," Connie said, "this wall is ready."

Taking the hammers, Dane and Wayne started at a seam and began to carefully pry off the plywood. After they took the first piece off, several more came off quickly. They laid them aside for later. Next they took out every other stud along the wall. They had to stop now and then to remove the electric boxes and wires. They ended up with eight pieces of plywood and twelve-eight foot studs. Then they started on the other side of the garage, just in case they would need the extra wood.

Frank grabbed the first few two-by-fours when they were ready and started marking the height they were going to be cut at. Then he marked the bottoms, so they could be cut to fit the holes in the back of the truck. Instead of cutting them to fit their width to fit the holes, they were going to fit them with the width going ninety degrees to the length of the truck bed. That would give them three and a half inches inside to inside for the walls.

Each person pitched in where they could in building the frame. One person would sit or stand on the wood while it was sticking out of the back of the bed, while someone else would cut the notch. After the first few boards, they got into the swing of it. They quickly had six boards ready to put in the holes on the back of the pickup.

Next they attached six horizontal boards at the top, all around the side walls, then one more in the center, across the top of the bed. It only took twenty minutes to cut and prepare a framed doorway for the back.

On both sides and in front and back they framed in small horizontally slotted windows for viewing, and to put a rifle barrel through.

After that was finished, they hauled one piece of plywood at a time and put it in the back of the bed. Then Frank drew out lines on it. They used the wood drill bits to start the cutouts for the small windows, and then used the small hand saw to cut them out. Before long they had all of the sides screwed together.

As the guys finished putting the walls on the inside and outside, the girls got the buckets and started filling them with dry dirt. Once the walls were ready, they would have the guys dump the dirt into the walls and compact it as best they could. It was exhausting work for all of them, except for Connie. She was used to hard work. After dozens of buckets of dirt, the ceiling was ready to install. It took twenty more buckets for the ceiling, then they screwed on the roof.

Exhausted, sweaty and dirty, they stood back and admired their work. The old work horse of a truck barely squatted with all the added weight. The shocks were heavy duty and were able to handle the weight. The six foot tall frame with slotted windows looked ready to take on an army. They would still have to protect the tires, glass windows and the engine compartment, but that would wait until after lunch.

When the food came out, so did Lucky, who seemed to be quite at home lounging under the truck despite the noise and activity.

"Four and a half inches of wood and dirt," Frank exclaimed. Damn fine idea Wayne. "Where did you get the idea?"

"I was thinking about driving through possible hostile areas, and wishing we could find an armored truck, and drive that around. Then I imagined how we could make one with the materials available, and this came to mind," he replied modestly.

"Oh honey ko, I'm so proud of you."

"Thanks sweetheart but you should be proud of everyone yourself included. Everybody did an excellent job. It will take a very high powered rifle to punch through that."

They all washed up as best they could and ate some elk jerky, raisin biscuits, and apples picked fresh the day before. They washed it down with cold well water. The clouds cleared up a little and resembled tufts of cotton, floating in the bright blue sky.

Lounging against a rear tire, Frank was gnawing on the last piece of jerky and commented, "Damn fine jerky, Connie. Do you have a secret recipe?"

Eyeing her father with a straight face, she replied, "Cow urine. I age it for several weeks, filter it and then age it a little more. I guess the uric acid adds a little twang to it.

Frank froze, then sat up quickly. He spit out his mouthful of jerky, then took a drink from his canteen, swished it around in his mouth and spit. Wiping his mouth with the back of his hand, he looked up in time to see Connie falling over from her sitting position. She started laughing so hard she had tears in her eyes. "Oh Dad, you should have seen the look on your face." She continued to laugh hysterically as she rolled onto her back, clutching her stomach. A few of the others laughed along with her, glad that she was just kidding. Lucky swooped in to get the unwanted tidbit.

After her hysterics slowed down a bit and Connie could breath again, she said, "Sorry Dad, I couldn't help it. As for the secret recipe I … actually use … horse pee…" and she was off on another fit of laughing and rolling on the ground. This time she had to hold her crotch, trying not to pee her pants. This was the opening for Frank to pounce on his daughter in revenge. He knew she was extremely ticklish and knew just where to get the best results. After a minute, Connie finally made it to her feet and fled to the nearest bush.

"Take that, you young wench," exclaimed her dad to her receding back. Everybody was laughing and wiping tears or holding their stomachs. It was the funniest thing they had seen in a long time.

After Connie returned and they resumed working on covering the tires, they would occasionally glance at each other and start giggling again.

Instead of using a dirt box to cover the tires, they decided on a hinged two ply cover. It was ingeniously simple. In front of the front and back wheel wells, they drilled a hole large enough for a half inch diameter bolt. They put two pieces of plywood on either side of the truck fender, and then ran a four-inch lag bolt through them. Frank cut out a three foot pear shaped piece of plywood with what looked like a small shark fin sticking out on the big end, arcing down. He then cut a hole for the lag bolt in the small part of the "pear". While he did that, Wayne drilled another hole aft of each wheel well and put another, smaller, bolt through to stop the back part of the moveable cover from hitting the ground. After cutting and fitting the first piece, Frank drew the outline for seven more pieces. It took them a few hours to manually cut them, but the assembly went quickly afterwards.

Dane went around and did a check on all four covers. They covered all but a few inches at the bottom. If they came to rough terrain and the front of the truck, or the bed, dipped too far, the covers would raise and lower to the terrain. They would be able to protect the tires without being set firmly in place, and possibly getting torn off.

The next project was windows, but they were all starting to get hungry again, so they decided to call it a day. They loaded up the extra plywood and studs, so they could finish the job at the shelter. To preventing her father from getting more revenge, Connie rode in the back.

They stopped at the Marshall's place to show Frank what they found. After showing him the working solar panels, the hot water and working propane stove, they took him in through the hidden door and down the stairs.

As Frank came down the stairs, he pointed to the hole built into the wall. "That looks like a good place to cover the steps from, smart."

"Were you in the military?" Dane asked.

"Yep, I spent two years in and around Da Nang.

"Holy crap," he exclaimed as he turned left at the wall. "Marshall must have been loaded to stockpile this much stuff. Have you looked through it all? There must be enough food and supplies to feed a small army."

"No, we've only scratched the surface. We've only taken a few things since we found it. We started leaving a trail here, so we decided to wait a while before going back. But, this is where we got the two-way radios. There were also chargers and rechargeable batteries. With electricity available, we've been able to keep them charged."

Narrowing his eyes slightly, he looked at Wayne. "You told me there was a stash of food and supplies, but damn! This is a big deal."

While they were talking and Dane was getting the radios off the chargers, the women searched for more chocolate. It only took about a half minute to find the buried treasure. "Chocolate," trilled Perra. As the women dove into their little bag of heaven, Dane looked through more of the boxes that tumbled over. "Figures," he said. "Take a look at this," he said to the two guys several feet to one side. He pulled out an unopened box. Inside it was a brand new Black and Decker skill saw, complete with an extra blade.

"You've got to be kidding," Frank responded. "We could have had the truck completely done today with a skill saw. Oh well, at least we'll have it for tomorrow. It shouldn't take very long to knock out the rest of it."

"You know," he continued, "We really need to inventory this stuff. There may be more important stuff buried right under our noses."

"Frank, I think you're right. Something that's been bugging me is that John said he was a hunter all of his life, but I haven't seen any rifles or ammunition."

Dane brought his head up and looked at his brother. "I should have thought of that. I remember you saying something about it when we first came down here, but it somehow skipped my mind."

"They are probably buried in here somewhere," said Frank, looking at the mountain of supplies.

"Why would he bury his weapons?" Dane asked.

"Good question, but *where* is what I'd like to know. Maybe he has a safe in here somewhere."

After poking around for a little while and chatting, they decided it could wait. They had several rifles with plenty of ammo already available, and they were tired from their day of unaccustomed work. They decided to close up and head back to their home to rest up for the remainder of the work tomorrow.

CHAPTER 13
SMOKE SIGNALS

During a hearty meal of canned elk, brown rice, home made gravy, canned carrots and homemade flat bread, topped off with honey cakes, they talked about their upcoming trip. The road leading south-west from the highway would pass many houses; too many to search safely. There were several miles of open road that they would have to drive before they got to town. They were divided on how best to search. Frank wanted to go in with the horn blaring, and anyone left alive would probably come out to greet them.

"That would definitely get peoples attention," said Dane, "but I don't think making ourselves a target is a good idea."

"Anybody left alive out there is probably looking for people just like us. I think that most of the really violent ones, are dead by now," retorted Frank.

"But if there are *enough* violent people left, they could shoot our wooden tank to pieces."

"I say it's a risk we need to take to find out if my grandson is still alive," Frank said heatedly.

"And I say your judgment is clouded *because* of your grandson, and it could get us all *killed!*" Dane replied as his face reddened with anger.

"What makes you the expert on searching for someone?" Frank spat back.

"Dad …calm down …" Connie interjected.

Dane suddenly pushed his mostly empty plate away, stood up and towered over Frank. His emotions firmly in control as he looked down, and replied in a hardened voice, "I served in Afghanistan several years ago. My convoy was ambushed, and several of my people were taken. We followed them into a small city. We didn't have a clue as to whether the people were hostile or not. Every corner we took, every window and door we passed, we had to check out. I lost two men just in the search. Even then it took us hours to track them down, and by the time we found them the guys had been butchered like pigs. The single woman among them had been raped and mutilated beyond any hope of a normal life." He stood there looking down with a glazed look in his eyes. He saw nothing but the memory of his former buddies. He turned and walked a few steps toward the stairs heading down and out to fresh air. Stopping and turning his head to the side, he continued in a muted voice that somehow seemed loud, "It's suicide to advertise ourselves to an unknown force. We know next to nothing about *anything* out there and I will *not* be put in that situation again."

They all heard him go down the metal stairs, open the inside door, then felt the airflow increase as he went out the outer door.

"It's not my fault he had a bad experience in the military," Frank said defiantly.

"He's right Dad. If we go in not knowing what's out there, then we could be asking for trouble. Despite the fact that we have something to help protect us from harm, any people out there may be afraid of our "wooden tank", as Dane called it, and start shooting. As much as I want to find Chris and other people, we're going to have to do it slowly. If he *is* alive, getting ourselves killed won't help him any." She patted her fathers hand affectionately, then followed Dane outside.

Wayne and Perra sat quietly watching the whole thing, surprised by the intensity of it all. It was the first real quarrel anyone had in the last two years.

"I'm afraid I'm going to have to agree with the others," said Wayne quietly. "My brother can be moody, but he's a brilliant tactician. He'd received several medals from the military before he retired."

"So what do you suggest? From what I've heard of the area it will take us weeks to go from place to place. We might have another month before snow starts to fall."

"Smoke signals."

"What?" Frank asked.

"We can light a large fire out in the open. There are plenty of dead trees from the super storm. We can haul a bunch of logs to a parking lot and light it. Anybody around will be able to see it from miles away."

"And we can be hidden quite a ways away to see if anyone shows up." Frank nodded in agreement. "Not bad Wayne, but there are a few weaknesses to your plan. One; if people are around, they may not see it. Two; they may see it, but not come in fear of a trick."

"It's the best shot we have of getting people to come out from such a large area. The place was sparsely populated in an area with rolling hills. Unless you know where to get an airplane, and know how to fly it, I can't think of any other way to get attention."

"Ok, I guess you're right." He paused for a few seconds, and then added, "I don't know why I got so upset. I think maybe it's because we haven't been doing much of anything to find Chris, or other people, since I got here. I guess I'm just anxious to get out there and start searching."

Before her husband could respond, Perra said to Frank, "I know how you feel. I have lots of family in the Philippines that I am desperate to hear from. Part of what we have been searching for is a radio…what kind is it, honey ko?"

Turning to his wife he said, "A ham radio."

"Ah,OK," he said. "In the right conditions those can go for thousands of miles, even half way around the world." Frank paused for a second then sighed. "I suppose I should go apologize to Dane."

Frank got up from the table and started down the stairs. He paused halfway down and asked, "What's up with your names anyway? Usually twins have names that rhyme," he said with raised eyebrows.

Wayne chuckled for a second. He had heard that many times over the years. "Our parents were named Cain and Jane. They had a sense of humor when they named the three of us with rhyming names. It sure caused some confusion when they would call us from far away."

"Three of you?" he asked.

"Our sister, Loraine, died when she was 24."

"Oh, sorry," he said as he continued down the stairs.

The husband and wife just looked at each other, and then started cleaning up the dinner dishes.

Early the next morning they packed up after another good breakfast. Dane and Frank had made amends the night before and were in fairly decent moods.

The trip to the Marshall's place only took about five minutes. They unloaded the few things they needed and started right in on building the window covers.

The night before they had left most of the supplies in the garage that, like the house, also had power. It was fortified concrete and had what Dane swore were blast doors. The only way in, that they could find, was with an electric button inside the house.

Wayne went down into the shelter and brought up the skill saw and got it ready. They started out by building two makeshift saw horses to make the work easier, since the back of the truck was no longer available.

Frank took charge of construction again began by measuring the side windows. Weight was starting to be a concern since they still needed five people to ride in the truck. Instead of bolting on the protection, they were going to wire it together. It would be easier to remove. They also decided to build it using the flat side of the stud, making it two and a half inches thick. The horizontal slit would be two inches high by twelve inches wide. It did not take very much dirt to compact into the narrow spaces. After completing both sides, Frank stepped back and critically eyeballed the work. The top of the door to the bottom was well covered. It would take less to punch through, but at least it was something.

Because of the curve, the front window posed more of a problem. He did not want to crack it with the weight of the wood, so he decided on simplifying the project by boxing the hood and front of the radiator in the same fashion as the doors. After the hood and top of the cab were covered, he boxed in the window. He had to put it a few inches out so it would not touch the glass. It was a lot of work putting in several-one inch slits in front of the drivers seat. Overall the slits were about three feet wide.

When everything was complete, they all stood back and surveyed their work. Dane, surprisingly, started humming the song to Gilligan's Isle. Evidently the blocky truck reminded him of the makeshift cart the castaways had built. Everyone started laughing and a few started singing the words to the old show.

Now that they were finally done, they sat down and ate a late lunch. Evidently one or both of the women had found some peanut butter and some canned jelly. They got it back to the shelter without saying anything about it. It was a delightful surprise, even though Wayne wished that instead of biscuits, they could have had good old fashioned soft bread. An even bigger surprise was when Perra pulled out a bottle of champagne. She and Connie must have been doing some serious digging in the shelter while the guys completed the front end of the truck.

"Now what?" Connie asked as she wiped crumbs from her chin.

"I think we should figure out who should ride where and what each of us should do in case of trouble," Dane replied. "Two up front and three in back," he continued.

"Why two in front?" Frank asked. I can drive this tank just about anywhere you want to go."

"In case you get hurt we need someone else to take over. Connie and I are probably the two best shots here, with Wayne coming in next. I don't mean to be offensive Frank, but can you still shoot?"

"I would rather drive," he said, without answering the question.

"OK. Perra, how would you feel about riding up front with Frank?

Looking to her husband for a few seconds, she said, "I will be okay up front."

They talked of different scenarios, and ways to deal with them. Mostly they just decided to stick to the basics in any emergency: evacuate as quickly and safely as possible. If they somehow got separated, they would head to the closest of several predetermined areas along the way.

After they cleaned up the mess from building the "Tank", Dane and Connie decided to walk back. Lucky was more than happy to go with them. The rest piled into the truck and headed back.

Wayne sat by the passenger window, and when he rolled it down, he could see much better than he expected. The light coming in was fairly adequate, but looking down during night time, they might have a hard time seeing the sides of the road. They did not plan to drive in the dark, but if they did, they would have to be careful.

They were all feeling a little anxious the next morning. They loaded up with supplies of food, water, weapons, ammunition and a first-aid kit. They also threw in three fold up chairs for those in back. The first thing they were going to do was stop by Connie's place, and then head out to the highway. This trip was mostly a scouting trip. They would just take it easy and see what they could see. They were in no hurry to blunder into any situation that they could not easily get out of.

This trip they decided to leave Lucky at home. He would be unhappy, but they did not want any distractions.

The place looked the same as they pulled up. Connie flung the door open and jumped out the back of the truck. They had pulled the tail gate off so that the people riding in the back could exit without help. She went in quickly and came out several seconds later. The place was still empty. She got back in and secured the door. Once the door closed, Frank headed out to the highway.

The road was still fairly good in most spots. It was grown over with weeds and a few small trees, which Frank ignored as he plowed right over them.

There was a frontage road that headed only north. Instead of driving a few miles north to the on ramp, he drove to a fairly good spot and just crossed over to the pavement. "Hold on," he said through the back window. "We're going through a ditch, and it might get a little bumpy back there." He angled the truck and made it through with hardly slowing down.

The big eight cylinder engine quickly picked up speed, despite the added weight. The 390 cubic inch motor had a Holley four barrel high performance carburetor and could handle much heavier loads. It hardly made any difference with the higher-octane gas being replaced with propane.

The next exit was only four or five miles down the road. Frank glided up the off ramp and turned right. The road curved to the left, passed a burned out gas station and hotel. He pulled off by the station, so they could survey the surrounding area. All three passengers in the back had binoculars and could see quite well.

"Do you see anything?" Frank asked. Sitting beside him, Perra could see several burned out buildings on the other side of the road that.

"I don't see anything moving, except for a few deer a

hundred yards to the west. If there are people here, I'm sure they would be stocking up on meat for the winter. Maybe we should stay here for a little bit and watch the deer. They will let us know if anyone else is around," said Wayne.

The deer had been grazing and lifted their heads as they heard the noise from the truck. They watched for half a minute before lowering their heads back down again.

Perra wished she was in back. The window slit was just a little too high for her to see much of anything, unless she pushed up with her hands and craned her neck. Frank had built them for his level of sight.

After about twenty minutes, they headed down the road for another good spot to stop. Frank drove up to a ransacked convenience store with a dirt parking lot. The windows were broken out, and a busted up car sat out front with flat tires. Weeds grew from around the tires. He pulled around back, so they could see the open areas better. Dotting the hills and plains were houses. Most of them did not have much of a roof left, and many had caved in walls.

"I think this would be a good place to light a cozy fire," said Dane.

"I thought we were going to wait," Connie stated.

"Why waste propane driving around when this place is perfect? If you look at the leaves on the trees, you can see that the wind is hardly blowing. The smoke will rise straight up," Dane said as he gestured with his hands open.

The morning dew was still fresh on the grass as they agreed to go ahead and try a smaller fire. If nobody showed, they would try a larger one the next day.

The massive storms that raged across the planet for several months had knocked over a quarter of the trees. None escaped losing branches, and they were everywhere. Within ten minutes, they dragged enough wood to stack several feet high, and covered 200 square feet of ground. Wayne pulled off some green branches to create more smoke while Connie and Perra brought out some old newspapers from inside the old store. Several of the larger logs were on the bottom, with smaller pieces throughout the pile. It did not take much for it to ignite.

Quickly jumping back into the truck, they drove about a quarter mile back down the road and drove into an open garage. The driveway was about two hundred feet long and ended at a detached garage. There were only inches to spare as the truck inched inside. Frank got out and closed the garage door as wisps of smoke started rising from the pile. They all climbed out of the truck and took up positions looking out the garage windows.

Within five minutes, they had a nice, smoky bonfire. The smoke rose up until it hit the thermal barrier, then started drifting off to the south east. It had to be at least three hundred feet high, thought Wayne.

They all waited patiently with their binoculars up. Perra was bored, and decided to go check out the house. There were not enough binoculars to go around, and she could not see outside anyway.

The fire roared and smoked and billowed out its signal. They waited and waited and eventually took breaks. Two or three people were always watching the roads leading to and from the fire.

Wayne stepped back after a while and stretched his back and neck. His arms were also tired from constantly holding up the binoculars. The only thing he had seen was a few birds speeding through the air. While shaking out his arms, he noticed Perra was not around. Thinking about it for a few seconds, he could not remember her saying anything for the last few hours. "Where's Perra?" He asked. Connie was the first to respond, "The last I saw of her she was heading into the house. I totally forgot about it." She looked slightly embarrassed.

Wayne immediately grabbed his rifle and headed towards the exit. Before he got to the door, Connie was right behind him with her rifle ready. The others continued their vigil.

Swinging the door inside the garage, he quickly peered out. There was a paved walkway leading from the garage to a side door on the house, not more than fifteen feet from him. They silently crossed to the house while each one covered opposite directions. Wayne slowly twisted the knob and opened the door soundlessly. They went into a laundry room and closed the door, weapons still up.

Amped up on adrenaline, Wayne had to stop and slow his breathing. While he was catching his breath, he moved up beside another doorway leading out of the laundry room. He could see about thirty feet straight ahead to another wall. It looked like an elegant living room. He peeked to the right and could see a dining table.

Whispering to Connie, he told her to stay close behind him, and that they were going into the dinning room. Connie merely nodded and stared at him with her bright eyes.

Wayne slowly went out and to the right of the doorway, rifle down but ready. A chandelier hung dark above an oak dinning table with six perfectly placed chairs. He continued on several steps and peeked around a wide doorway to the left. An expensive kitchen with stainless steel utensils hanging over an island came into view. He did not waste time and continued through it to a large family room.

They stopped for several seconds and listened. They heard nothing but their own breathing. Wayne could see a bedroom from where he was standing and slowly went forward. He edged up to the doorway and slowly peeked inside. The room, like the others, looked immaculate and expensively done, but there was no sign of Perra. He continued on, fearful for his wife. His heart refused to slow down as he continued passed the room to the next one. It too was empty. With his heart pounding nearly out of his chest, he came to a six paneled mahogany door. It was closed, and when he tried the knob it was unlocked.

A hand suddenly grabbed his shoulder and nearly made him jump out of his boots. Connie smiled apologetically and whispered, "I think I heard something in that room over there." She did not wait for him as she stepped across the hallway to the closed door. She quickly grabbed the handle and pushed the door open. They quickly stepped in one after the other with their weapons ready.

The bathroom was just as orderly as the other rooms in the house, except for one thing. The small window high over the tub was open, and the small curtain was moving with the breeze.

Wayne turned to Connie in amazement. "You heard that?" He whispered incredulously. She simply shrugged her shoulders.

They headed back out into the hallway and to the fancy door. Quietly pushing the door open, they stepped into another, even more, elaborate bedroom. This time the bed was not made. Upon a closer look, they could see dark hair sticking out between a large pillow and a thick down comforter. Connie covered the room as Wayne quickly crossed to the bed and slowly pulled the covers back. His heart nearly leapt from his chest in relief as he realized that Perra was soundly sleeping.

Connie went around the four poster, king size bed to cover the door. She watched Wayne's face go through several emotions in a brief period as he stood there watching his sleeping wife. He tried to say something, but his throat seemed unable to cooperate. Connie lowered her weapon, walked around the bed and out the door, quietly closing it behind her.

Ten minutes later Wayne and Perra came out of the house and back into the garage, where Wayne silently took up his vigil. Perra, with reddened eyes, sat quietly on a stool near a work bench and pouted.

After a few more hours, the wood was gone, and the remaining pile of coals glowed hotly. They did not see anyone come out to check on the fire, so they all loaded back in the truck and drove up to the remnants. Those in back had a good vantage point, but saw no indication that anyone had come by.

The trip back was subdued as they each considered the implications. They all figured there would have been *someone* in all of those many acres of open range properties.

Lucky was wagging his tail with his whole body as they opened the shelter from the false wall. After a few licks to whomever was closest, he dashed outside for some immediate relief of a full bladder.

Wayne was still upset at his wife, but so very glad that she was okay. After waking her up from her restful slumber and giving her a hug, he chewed her out for the first time in their married life. He did not let up even after she broke down and apologized. He just *could not* lose her, and made sure she would *never* do anything like that again.

By sunrise the next day they were all up and ready to go. This time they were going to take Lucky. Perra, the superstitious one, said that ever since Lucky came into their lives, they had been remarkably lucky and that he would bring them luck this time. Wayne silently hoped so.

The trip was uneventful as they made their way back to the scorched parking lot. This time they used the truck to pull larger trees and branches. They pulled them as close together as they could, then built a small ramp so they could pull the next batch across the first layer. After that, they brought in tree limbs that required two people to move them. They kept stacking as high as they could, using green branches and limbs here and there.

Dane nearly broke his leg when he was trying to throw a large branch up to the top of the pile. He stepped on what he thought was solid footing, but as his weight shifted, so did the log on which he was standing. He let out a holler as he toppled sideways. His left foot caught between two logs as he fell. He instinctively reached out and was able to grab hold of a branch before he went too far.

"Hold on," said Wayne, who was near by and helped extricate his brother. Using his shoulder under his taller brothers arm pit, he helped him limp over to the truck. Pulling up his pant leg, they could see that the skin was not broken, but above the ankle, it was swelling and developing a nasty bruise. More than likely, he received a hairline fracture.

"That was close," Dane said as he sat in the cab of the truck rubbing his leg.

"Oh, you just wanted to get out of work," his younger brother joked.

"Yeah, I guess it worked," Dane replied with a grimace.

"That's all right, ten or fifteen minutes more and this beast will be ready to light.

Done at last, they added lots of paper and lit it from several places. The pile was almost fifteen feet high and twenty feet wide.

"I hope it works this time," said a sweaty and tired Frank. "I don't think we can do any better than that," he said as he pointed with a gnarled finger.

This time Frank backed into the garage, then got out and pulled the door down.

Perra made sure she got a set of binoculars, and something to stand on top of. She was not going to fall asleep this time.

The pile quickly built up a nice flame with lots of smoke. It took about a half hour for it to fully engulf all of the wood in the pile.

"*That* ought to get someone's attention," said Dane as he craned his head back, looking at the pillar of smoke.

"We'll see," Wayne said quietly.

Once again they ended up taking turns watching for any movement on the roads. Frank brought out a pack of playing cards and played a game of speed with Perra.

By the time it was getting dark, the blaze had died down to a large pile of coal. Dispirited, they headed back home. Frank, despite the other two guys telling him that he shouldn't, stubbornly drove home with his lights shining brightly. *To hell with it*, he thought. *We'll never find anybody if we keep trying to hide*. He did capitulate once he turned off the highway and onto the dirt road. There was no sense in getting stupid with his stubborn streak.

Once they unloaded their few supplies, they discussed their next move. They were fairly confident that if anyone could see the smoke that curiosity would have got the better of them and checked it out. Either they were too cautious or nobody was around. The next day they determined that they would push pass the small town of Colorado City and head for Rye. After that they would head to the reservoir and check on the houses there.

A while later, as Perra and Wayne were preparing dinner, Wayne looked down at Lucky and said, "Well, you aren't so lucky are you?" The dog simply sat there with his big brown eyes and wagged his tail uncertainly.

CHAPTER 14
WHERE IS EVERYBODY?

Frank soon tired of driving, and wanted to be able to look out from a higher vantage point. The leaves were turning varying shades of yellows, oranges, browns and reds. He looked forward to being in the back of the truck, and anticipated fresh air coming through the small window. He had not realized how many Aspens there were in this part of the state and loved their shimmering fall colors.

Lucky left prints on the frosty ground that morning as they headed off to their next destination. Wayne was afraid that they were getting complacent since they had not seen anyone for a long time. He saw how everyone, including himself, no longer carried their weapons the same way. Now it seemed more habit than a necessity. They even started to burn wood in their small stove during the day time, to take off the new coolness in the air. They felt fairly secure now that there was no response to their smoke signals. *Still,* Wayne thought, *all it takes is one person to get lazy, and then something's going to happen.* As an after thought, he grabbed the four radios.

Dane was driving this time around because of his leg. He did not like the limited view he had, but there was not too much in the road that he had to avoid. He actually liked the feel of driving again. It gave him a sense of freedom he had not felt in a long time. Although it was cold outside, he rolled his window all the way down so he could feel the wind blow his scraggly long hair. The wooden armor slowed most of the wind from coming in the window and made a whistling sound. Perra gave him a sharp look as the inside temperature dropped. Dane hardly noticed as she reached over and turned up the heater.

Turning off the highway, they passed the spot where they had seen the deer. This time there was a large buck with several well fed does. They trotted off as the truck sped by.

They stopped at the large pile of debris left over from their fire. It was still warm near the center. They could not see any evidence that anyone showed up at the fire. Anyone coming to see it would be able to tell it was set on purpose.

After they loaded up, Dane headed on down the road. He stopped a half mile away and came back, after they realized they left the dog. Lucky came bounding up, tail wagging furiously.

Dane drove down the road much slower than last time, so the people in the back could check out all the houses, near and far.

"Where the hell did everybody go?" Wayne asked. "They *all* can't be gone. *Some*one should have stocked up on food!" He exclaimed. Nobody replied as they all continued to search house after house with their binoculars.

Driving into the small town of Rye, Dane pulled over at a school. It was mostly burned to the ground. Rusted swing sets stood like long abandoned skeletons. Avenging teens must have gotten the last laugh at the historical old buildings. The modern school on the other side of the road fared no better.

There were many houses behind the first school, to the left of the road. Many of them were burned, along with many of the old trees shading them. The deadened sprawl of lone tree trunks stood watch over generations of lost homes and forgotten memories. There was no need to spend much time here, so they quickly and quietly got back in the truck and headed up the road leading into the mountains.

The further they went up into the mountains, the more they could see signs of violence. Cars, trucks and RV's were either crashed or burned out. They passed hundreds of vehicles within a few miles. It appeared that the ones that got stalled in the road had been hijacked, ransacked and then pushed off the road. There were piles of vehicles at the bottom of several ravines.

"Survivors must have come up here in droves," Wayne said as he looked out at all of the carnage. He saw skeletons, or at least parts of them, here and there.

"Looks like one hell of a fight," replied his brother. "Whatever you do Dane, don't stop for anything."

Regardless of the warning, they had to stop several times to move trees, limbs, and vehicles before they could continue. The road, in places, had almost been thoroughly covered with mudslides. Lucky for them, it had been dry for the last few weeks, so they got out and turned the front hubs for four wheel drive. Only once did they have to get out and cut trees out of their way. After that, the road was surprisingly clear. The mudslide must have happened before most of the vehicles got trapped.

The twisting and turning road finally brought them to the

last turn in the road before the reservoir. A few of the houses near the road were smashed from falling trees.

Wayne topped the hill and saw an empty lake. Not only was it empty, but the road leading across the dam was washed out. He drove down the road and stopped several yards away from the gaping chasm.

They all unloaded to get a better look at the catastrophe. The hills behind the small reservoir were bouncing back from a massive mudslide. The terrible storm that racked the area soaked the dirt so much that the whole side of the mountain sloughed into the water. The small tidal wave had been too much for the earthen dam, and sent it roaring down the valley below.

Lucky happily chased after a fat squirrel.

"So much for San Isabel," Wayne said sadly as he shook his head. He could see a few boats sticking out of the ground. Vegetation grew all over the undulating mess. There were pools of stagnant water here and there. None of them were very big. Surprisingly, a few saplings reached several feet tall. The place was rich in organic material, and thick in places with shrubs and grass.

"Now what," Connie asked miserably. She could just picture her son cuddled up with his girlfriend in a nice, warm house on the other side. "It'll take hours to back track and drive around to the other side."

Wayne carefully climbed up on top of the truck and looked at the far side of the reservoir, where a road used to go around the water. "Maybe not," he said after a minute. Connie, and then Frank, climbed up and took up the same posture. It was about a mile to the north-west.

Someone had made a trail, no, a road through the twisted

trees and lumped up earth. It was very vague, but noticeable with their binoculars.

"Yes," exclaimed Connie. "A way through, but, who made that road? It looks really rough from here. Do you think we can get to the other side?" She asked no one in particular.

Climbing down, Wayne said, "One way to find out. We came here looking for people, so we might as well keep going. We still have several hours of light," he said looking at the sky.

Dane made sure everyone was loaded in, then turned around and headed up the road a short way and made a right turn. He had to gun it going over some moist ground. It built up over a low area of the pavement, but he soon made it to the other side.

"Hey, you want to warn us next time," came a voice from the back. A barely audible "sorry", came back.

The going got rough after a quarter mile. The paved road disappeared under the run off from the mountain. They could see some tire marks that lead into the rougher parts. They were not fresh, but they were not old either. Dane stopped the truck, got out and hobbled up to their first obstacle. A fallen tree had dirt piled up on both sides of it. Someone went to lots of trouble to get passed it.

"Whoever did this has a shorter wheel base than we do," Connie said. "I know my truck, and with this load, we'll be scraping the bottom before we get half way over."

Wayne stepped back to the back of the truck and returned with two shovels. "One way to fix that," he said as he handed her a shovel.

Connie eyed him and the offered shovel for a few seconds, then nodded, and started shoveling dirt to extend the mound.

Twenty minutes later they had extended their pathway

three feet on each side. The dirt and grass came up easy enough, but the thinner air had them both passing the shovels after about five minutes. Frank and Perra gladly jumped in, happy to be doing something constructive.

To keep from getting stuck in the new dirt, they started jumping up and down or stomping their feet to compact it. That got them breathing even harder than the shoveling.

Dane sat in the truck pointedly rubbing his sore spot.

"Ok Dane, it's ready for you to drive over. Let's hope it works. We can push if it looks like you're going to get stuck," said Connie.

Unhappy at not being able to see the ground in front and to the sides of him, Dane started up the truck and inched it forward. The tires sank a few inches, but the truck did not slow down. The sliding protection on the back wheels slowly rose up, then back down as he made it safely over the tree.

"Take that you stupid tree," said Connie as she high-fived Wayne. They loaded back in and continued on their bumpy ride across the dirt road.

The road was barely that. It had been used several times, but not recently. There were no bent or broken blades of grass, bushes or trees. In some places the ruts were deep, but not too deep for the truck. The only trees in the path were small, and they could see where many saplings had been cut down. Many places along the way the pathway snaked around busted trees almost as large as a small tire.

A loud hissing noise suddenly came from outside the truck. Dane stopped and opened his door in time to see the rear tire flattening quickly.

"Damn it," he exclaimed loudly. Limping back to the mortally wounded tire, he saw a piece of sharp metal sticking out of the ground. The last turn he made must have just missed the front tire.

As if in mourning, they all stood looking at the tire. "No problemo," said Connie, suddenly bright. I always keep two spare tires. I can't remember how many times I've had to change out a tire when out in the fields. Only once before have I had to change out two."

They got out one of the spare tires along with the jack and lug wrench. To access the tire, they simply lifted up the plywood cover. The jack kept sinking into the ground, so they lowered the truck back down, pulled the jack out, threw a few rocks in the hole, and then tried again. It sank a few inches, and then started raising the truck. Within five minutes, they were on their way again. Dane drove more carefully this time.

After forty-five minutes they finally made it around the wounded landscape. The paved road emerged from the hillside and continued on with many houses on either side.

Dane stopped in the middle of the road, so they could rest for a while. Even though he had gone slowly, the jostling took its toll on backs, legs and arms. A few bumps on some foreheads were also evident.

"I'm not looking forward to the trip back," said Frank as he rubbed a noticeable bump on his own forehead.

"Me too," said Dane, whose neck was sore from craning it high enough to see closer to the truck. His left hip and side were also sore from the radio digging in every time he got jostled too much.

"Who's up for a nap," Perra joked. A steely eyed look came from Wayne. She lowered her head, but his eyes started to shine with a smile, and her head came back up.

"These houses look like they weathered the storm fairly

well," announced Frank. Suddenly interested again, they all got out and surveyed their surroundings. About half of the houses ended up wiped out from the landslide, but of the others that survived, they looked to be in reasonable shape. Some of them even had shutters on the windows, and a few were boarded up. Only a few trees were growing between the houses, and a few had fallen. One fell squarely in the middle of a garage. Peering into the V-shaped garage, a solitary vintage headlight stuck out from its former safe place.

"I don't like being this exposed," said Dane. "We have nowhere to fall back to. Nowhere quick, I mean. Anyone around would have seen us making our way here."

"If anyone were here, don't you think they would have sent a welcoming committee?" Frank asked as he looked around. Even though he and Dane made amends, he could not help verbally poking him in the ribs once in a while.

"Maybe," said Connie, intervening. "Maybe they are checking us out to see what we are up to. Look at it from their point of view. We show up in their neighborhood in a make shift tank with weapons. What would you do, Dad?"

With the jab returned, but from another direction, he just stood and pondered for several seconds. "I'd probably stay hidden until I knew their intentions. I don't think anyone this far away would have seen our smoke signals either," he said as an after thought.

They loaded up and headed down the road, driving slowly. They were silent as the truck ambled down the old road.

An old trading post on the right did not weather the storm as well as most buildings. To the right of the fallen store, old paddle boats lay askew on the dried up bed of the sloping inlet where they had been lined up for rent.

Wayne had his brother stop for a minute while he checked the store for anything useful. Just minor goods that were not needed for survival were all that remained. Lots of dust, mud, and debris clogged the outer areas of the caved in old wood building.

The only restaurant around was on the left side of the road, on a corner that sat on an angle facing the road that used to go across the dam. Dane pulled into the dirt parking lot, so they could survey the area, and then eat lunch. There was a strange mix to the small town that made him uneasy. There were buildings that looked as if they were maintained, while others were obviously run down and abandoned. The roads were clear of large debris, but not of smaller leaves and branches. Several of the vehicles had been scavenged, mostly for tires, while a few looked ready to drive.

They all sensed something weird about the town, but put it down to jangled nerves from the bumpy ride. Still, they kept their weapons closer than usual.

They took turns using the binoculars, checking out the houses nearby. After nearly a half hour, they finally relaxed and decided to head into the restaurant for their meal. The women carried their food and drinks while Wayne carried their weapons and a few other supplies inside.

"What's the matter Lucky," Connie asked, as she carried the large package of bread, canned fruits, vegetables and dried meat, "are you tired too?"

The place was small and well organized, but just a little dusty. The pictures and antiques on the rough-hewn walls spoke of the local history and gave the place an air of the early pioneer days.

Connie spread a large towel over one of the tables in a

booth before bringing out the food. She laid everything out while Perra brought out some Apple cider and utensils. Wayne brought in a load, set it down, then set his weapon against a neighboring booth. Frank quickly wiped down the seats. The others placed their weapons with Waynes, as well. Dane shouldered his rifle and did a short walk through looking for a bathroom.

The small, dark restroom had a toilet, one urinal and a sink with the usual mirror and a wall mounted towel dispenser. Dane was not too surprised when he tested the faucet and water splashed into the sink. It was refreshingly cold as he splashed water on his face. He had hoped that the water would shake him from the uneasy feeling he had since he first drove up to the graveyard of burned out vehicles, earlier that morning. He felt much better after the cold shock of the high-altitude water. Instead of returning to the mouth-watering meal right away, he decided to take quick toilet break. Just before he let go a stream, he noticed all of the talking in the other room had stopped.

The food was laid out self serve style. Wayne and Perra grabbed their food right away and sat down to eat. Lucky looked at them expectantly, then suddenly looked into the kitchen, where a man was standing with a rifle at the high ready position.

Chapter 15
The Cost of Complacency

"Please don't move," announced the darkened shadow, just loud enough to stop everyone in their tracks. "Where did you come from?" He asked in the same smooth, deep voice.

A flash of anger and panic made Wayne's jaw grind as he realized their mistake. They had checked out all of the houses with binoculars and saw nothing, no smoke; nothing. Regardless, they failed to fully check out the building in which they were going to take a break. He seethed with anger at his own stupidity, knowing this was the mistake he was afraid they would make. He had expected it of some of the others, but not himself. As casually as he could, he said, "We came from down by the Interstate."

Their weapons were all stacked together against the next booth, between them and the stranger in the darkened hallway leading to the kitchen.

"Why are you here?"

"We're looking for other people. We've been isolated for a long time and haven't found anyone else alive."

The weapon lowered a few inches, then, "how many of you are there?"

"Just the five of us," answered Wayne.

"Where is the fifth?"

Wayne did not hesitate as he pointed down at Lucky. "He's right there."

Lucky had his head lowered and his tail down. His hackles raised slightly at the tension coming from the people around him.

The man suddenly lowered his rifle. He seemed to force a smile and came forward.

"Welcome to the Commonwealth of San Isabel." He shot his hand out.

"My name is Jose."

"I'm sorry if I scared you, but we keep getting raided a few times per week. It's been going on for the past few months, and we never know when we are going to be hit again." He smoothly shouldered his rifle.

"Raided? By whom, and... I'm sorry. My name is Wayne, and this is my wife Perra. That's Connie and her father Frank," he said pointing.

Frank studied the stranger and was unusually quiet. He did not like the forced smile the man had briefly showed. He offered his hand as he was introduced, but said nothing.

The stout Mexican warily eyed the dog, then the food on the table with a watering mouth. "There are about sixty of us living in the hills a few miles from here. This town was too open to keep us protected, so we moved to a place more secure. Since we kept getting our supplies stolen by a bunch of thieves, we deserted this place. It's my turn to stand guard out here. I was relaxing when I heard you guys come in the front door.

Don't tell anyone I was sleeping on the job, huh?" He said with that forced smile again.

Perra saw him looking at the food and asked him if he were hungry. He licked his lips and said, "That looks really good. Yes, if you have enough."

Wayne reached in the box that the dishes came in and handed it to his wife. Jose's eyes narrowed at the extra plate. "How come you have an extra plate?" He asked casually.

"Lucky is a little spoiled. We give him the scraps after we're through eating," Connie added.

With his eyes on the savory food, he said, "Lucky really *is* lucky to be eating this good," he said before taking a bite of the canned fruit.

"So you stand guard all alone while everyone else stays at your town? That sounds boring," Perra said as she watched Jose wolf down the fruit and vegetables.

"Not really a town as much as a small village," he said after swallowing a large portion. "Where did you get the fruit?"

"We found it in an abandoned house way back in the woods," lied Frank. "That's the last of it."

Jose just nodded his head as he licked his fingers. Without any offered silverware, he had dug into his food with his fingers. "Ah, elk jerky," he said as he took a small bite. "We have plenty of this, but the fruit and veggies... um..um."

"The Boss is going to want to meet you folks," he said after a few seconds. "I'm sure you have lots of questions too. My relief should be here in another few minutes or so."

Wayne was painfully aware of how close Jose was to the rifles. Out of the corner of his eye he could see Dane peeking around the corner. He very subtly put his right hand out of sight of Jose, but to where his brother could see. He made the "retreat" sign and his brother's head slowly disappeared.

"How long do you have to stay here?" Perra asked innocently.

Jose wiped his mouth with his sleeve before he answered, "Only one night. We're supposed to fast while were out here. It's supposed to clear the mind and body. I think it's mostly to save on food. We're posted here mostly to see if anyone drives up the road." Realizing he was probably saying too much, he changed the subject.

Looking out the front window, he asked, "What in the Mother's Name is that?" He was looking at the truck decked out in its wooden armor.

"We didn't know what to expect, so we tried to protect the truck with a little wood framing," said Frank, who was decidedly uneasy around this strange man.

"Looks kind of intimidating to me," he said in a strange voice.

Changing the subject on purpose, Wayne asked, "So tell us about your Commonwealth. Why are there so few of you with all of these houses here?"

"It's a long story, but after the "Fall of Man", many of the people that showed up out here were...kind of crazy...and...well, many of them didn't...make it. It was a mess, with all those people and so little food to go around. When the storms came and took out the reservoir it got worse. We ended up isolated, but people kept showing up and...well, maybe the Boss should tell you about it."

A jeep pulled up outside, and four armed men got out. Wayne knew he should have listened to his gut, clobbered Jose, and got out while the getting was good.

They filed in quickly with weapons at the half ready position. "About time you guys got here," Jose complained. "Sorry, but false alarm." He backed up a few feet but did nothing more. "Well folks, are you ready to meet the Boss?" He asked with a weird smile.

"There may be another one here," he said to them. "Check the place out." Two men quietly and efficiently proceeded down the other hall, where the bathrooms and storage rooms were. A younger man walked over and grabbed their weapons. "Sorry folks, but until the Boss tells me otherwise; I will need to secure your firearms. And uh, thanks for the food."

Perra's eyes suddenly teared up as she said in her little girl voice, "What are you doing? We haven't done anything. We just want to meet other people and find out if anyone has a pork, er...ham radio so I can talk to my family." She nearly sobbed as her husband stepped over to her and took her in his arms.

"Don't worry little lady, you'll fit in nicely after the Boss checks you out. We don't want anyone to hurt anyone else, so just come along quietly and we'll all have a pleasant day.

Frank and Wayne both were bristling at the slimy bastard's smooth, and at the same time oily, voice.

The two men that had disappeared down the hall came back empty handed. "Nobody else is here Jose. You must be getting antsy sitting out here by yourself."

Connie had trained Lucky well. Besides training him to fetch, sit, heel and point, she also trained him to hide. It was a little game she played with him when they had the time. It was hilarious to see him run and hide, waiting to be found. He got a yummy treat every time she found him.

Connie raised her right finger and wagged it around.

Lucky picked up on the hand gesture and took off on a dead run. She hated to send him off, since she would not be able to follow him. She was not sure how long he would wait until he returned, but it was better than letting these men get a hold of him. She would not have been surprised if he would have ended up as dinner.

The younger man twirled and aimed at the dog. Connie sent a well-placed kick to the back of his knee, and sent him sprawling. He was up in an instant, but the dog was gone. His face was livid as he advanced on Connie.

"Knock it off Tony," Jose said as he stepped between the two. "You can't blame the lady for trying to protect her dog. Besides, we've been a little rude to these people. They aren't the ones that have been stealing from us. I can tell by the food they have, and none of it resembles anything we've been missing."

"Try that again lady, and you'll lose a tooth." He slung his rifle over his shoulder and stomped out the door. The weapons on his other shoulder clattered loudly.

Jose turned to the strangers and raised both of his hands. "Sorry folks, this has been a case of mistaken identity. As soon as you showed up, I called for back up," he said as he patted a radio on his hip. "I'm glad to see some new faces."

"Can we have our weapons back?" Frank asked. "I feel naked without mine."

"If you don't mind, I'll have to ask the Boss when we get back home. He doesn't allow any weapons unless we are on watch or hunting. I'm sure you can understand."

"I understand you've taken our only way to protect ourselves," Wayne said as rationally as he could.

"Well, you claim that you want to meet other people, right?"

"Yes, *peaceful* people."

"With a ham radio," added Perra.

"Then I'm sure you will realize that any peaceful groups around will have their rules to follow, right?"

Wayne was still very uncomfortable with the turn of events. Something was still not right, even though Jose and his friends had all shouldered their weapons and took easier postures. He could see that arguing would only compound things, so he decided to lay low and try to contact his brother covertly if things got worse.

Jose was watching him carefully and could see the acceptance come over him.

"Great, let's go. You won't mind if I drive, do you?"

Connie had, for the last several years, kept a second key on her, after she ended up locking herself out of her own truck several times. At a time like this, she was glad that she did. Dane had the other key with him.

CHAPTER 16
HIDE AND SEEK

As Dane melted into the dark hallway, a quick search revealed a ceiling access panel. The bathroom and hallway had been darker than the rest of the building, so his eyes were already adapted. An antique book shelf was along the wall, so he slowly climbed high enough to push the panel up and to the side. Dust fell and almost made him sneeze. He grabbed a hold of one side and pulled himself up. Although he had been careful, he left a few small toe prints on two of the shelves. He grabbed the lid and scraped some dust off then quietly blew it down and in the direction of the shelves. It helped some and no longer looked fresh. There was nothing he could do now but hope the darkness would conceal it. He just got the lid back down when he heard the squeaking of some brakes outside. Dusty beams of light streamed in from a few vents on each end of the attic, so he was able to see. There were lots of antiques, but he found nothing helpful. He hoped nobody came up, because the only way to hide was to climb under something terribly dusty. Already his sinuses were swelling up. *I'm getting too old for this shit* he said to himself.

The voices below were barely audible as he sat on a dusty old chest. He looked around, then slowly made his way to one of the vents and looked out. He could not see much since the slats were close together and pointed down at a sharp angle. Working as quietly as possible, he pried a few loose to could get a better view. He saw one young guy come out of the building thoroughly pissed off. He put four rifles in the back, then climbed into the driver's seat of the Jeep and just sat there fuming.

The rest of the group soon came out carrying their supplies. "Damn it," he quietly exclaimed. Three men came out behind them, carrying their weapons with the barrels pointed down. Dane was somewhat confused. They were not tied up, or even had any weapons pointed at them. They seemed uncomfortable, but did not look as if they were forced into going. *What the hell is going on*? he asked himself.

Wayne got in the passenger seat while the big Mexican got in on the driver's side. The others willingly got in the back of their truck. Dane waited patiently while the truck backed up and headed away from the broken dam. The jeep followed right behind.

Dane saw no purpose to staying where he was. He needed to find out where they went. He wasted no time in getting back out of the attic, but made sure he left no sign that he had been there. Once out, he checked his gear and assessed his situation. He had his rifle with two clips full of ammunition. He had his radio, which he turned on to see if he could hear anything, then turned it down low. He pulled off his small back pack and checked the contents. He had a small medical kit, a small LED flashlight that you shook to create energy for light, binoculars, a multi-tool on his belt, a canteen mostly full, and a P38, which was a military version of a can opener. With his inventory complete, he reloaded his meager supplies into his small backpack. His stomach grumbled as he looked at where his lunch had been.

He headed to the still open door and made sure nobody was around. He decided to keep his radio down low, just in case someone in the back of their truck tried to reach him. He waited a few minutes, then headed out and to the side of the building. The land dropped off on the other side of the road, and at the bottom there was a trail that used to lead to some houses in the little valley below. He hoped they were still there. He certainly did not want to waste energy going down the hill since it would take up precious time. Instead, he decided to travel along that side of the road and would use the valley as a place to hide if anyone came along.

Moving as quickly as he could on his sore leg, he only went a few hundred feet when he heard something behind him. It was moving fast. Spinning around and bringing up his rifle, he thumbed off his safety as he aimed at the blur that was coming at him. With barely a millisecond to spare, he recognized Lucky and eased off the trigger. "What the hell are you doing here?" He asked the dog. Lucky was panting and was wet from the belly down. Dane had not realized that the dog did not leave with everyone else. It was not like Connie to let the dog run wild in an unknown area. *What the hell is going on?* He thought again.

CHAPTER 17
THE COMMONWEALTH

They pulled off to the left of the road and drove up a dirt road. Wayne still had his radio on his hip, but he did not dare turn it on in case the radio traffic revealed their hidden partner. He did not think Dane would be that stupid, and figured there would be time to contact him later.

As Jose drove up the road, Wayne could see motor homes, camper trailers and shacks built into a huge circle. The oddball arrangement made an effective barrier. Outside of that barrier they had another one under construction that must have taken considerable effort to construct. Logs were de-limbed, de-barked, then placed upright into a narrow, four feet deep pit that went entirely around their camp. People were tamping dirt and rocks back down into the ditch after they lined up several logs in a row. The tops were about fifteen feet high and very pointed. There were people drilling holes on each pole, a few feet from the top and another one about half way down. On one side of each pole, they were pounding in wooden dowels. It was obvious that it was to keep them lined up together. The main draw back was that the trees tapered as they went up, leaving gaps between them. Anyone could look in, but, on the other hand, anyone could look out. Wayne was not sure how long the trees would stand like that before they rotted and fell. As of now, it was extremely imposing.

"Welcome to our home. I know it looks rough, but there are some good people here, and we all do our share to contribute."

As Jose drove up to the barricade, a few people laid some heavy planks over the ditch. He carefully drove over them, around a large garden spot in the center, and into an open carport. There were two other trucks that looked as if they were in decent shape. A large motor home butted up against one end of the building. Another, smaller carport, was on the other end with two vehicles inside.

Everyone emerged from the truck and gathered together. A tall, thin man came striding over to them with a purpose to his step.

"Welcome to my Commonwealth," he said through crooked teeth, one of them busted off at an angle. "You can call me Boss." He extended a work roughened hand and shook the newcomer's hands. Where did you fine folks come from?" He asked quickly.

"From down by Interstate 25," Wayne said.

"Oh, are you from Colorado City? Pueblo? No? Rye? How about Walsenburg?"

Wayne hardly had time to answer before the next question was fired at him. "We live to the East of the highway, on Thatcher Ranch," he lied.

"Come, please, we have much to discuss. I run this place and bring order to the chaos that has fallen upon us," he said in an almost sing-song fashion, much like a preacher spreading his message to his flock. He started walking to an expensive looking motor home. It looked to be about 45 feet long and had two slide-out sections that they could see.

The other men drifted off to their previous duties, while Jose gathered up the weapons, and took them to what looked like an armored truck. An unarmed guard unlocked the back door. He stowed all of their rifles, except one, in slots made for them. Jose shouldered the remaining rifle and left as the guard re-locked the truck.

He spied his replacement and approached him. They talked for a few minutes, then headed to the Jeep and drove back to the abandoned town.

CHAPTER 18
LUNCH FOR TWO

Dane could hear a vehicle coming before it got around the corner. He quickly stepped off the side of the road and headed down a steep hill. Lucky followed promptly, and seemed to think it was a game. The leaves that coated the grassy hillside made it slippery. Dane slipped a few times but, luckily, did not hurt his leg any more. He continued down the slope by grabbing a hold of the trees. Once he reached the bottom he continued on in the same direction that the road was going. He knew there were houses down here from when he came out to visit the castle. It was being built much further up the road. There was no sign of any of the flood water that had ravaged the valley going the other way. He was heading slightly up hill along the valley when he found a trail. It was a well-worn trail that looked as if it had been used for many years.

"What you think Lucky? Do you think we should stick to the trail?" He asked as he looked around. Lucky just looked at him with his big brown eyes and romped around some more.

"Okay, I guess we'll use the trail, but you keep an eye out," he admonished the playful dog.

They kept to the path and, after a half mile, Dane could see some houses. A few had some windows broken out, but otherwise looked intact. He decided to leave the trail and head to the closest house. "Heel, Lucky," he said quietly. The dog immediately came to his left side and looked up at him. As a reward, he scratched behind one ear. He got a small wag of the tail in return.

They slowly approached a two-story house that faced the trail. The hill behind it was not as steep or as high now, but he still had a hard time seeing where the road was.

"Down, Lucky," he commanded. "Stay," he said as Lucky lay down in the wild grass. He laid there looking at Dane expectantly. There were no treats to reward him with, so he gave him another scratch behind the other ear.

Treading lightly he went around the back of the house. Peering into a window, he could see that the place was completely bare. There were no window shades, no furniture; nothing. He carefully tried the door knob and found it locked. He tried a few of the windows and found one of them unlocked, so he quietly climbed inside. He checked the whole house and found the same as downstairs, so he went to the back door, unlocked it, then called Lucky to him. He wanted somewhere that he could keep the dog from giving away his presence. After he let the dog in, he went upstairs and used his binoculars to check out the other houses grouped in his general vicinity.

There was an oddball group of houses clumped together that ranged from very old to fairly new. The oldest looked to be made of thick timbers with stucco between the horizontal creases. It canted several degrees to one side, but looked as if someone had been living in it. There were still curtains in the unbroken windows. The newest looked used, but much more modern materials had been used in its construction. Several of the others looked somewhat dilapidated.

He did not want to have to spend much time here, but he was getting hungry and needed to find his family. He knew he would not be of much help being low on energy, so he decided to make a quick walkthrough of the other houses, just in case any food was left. He did not dare shoot anything, as it would give away his presence.

He went out the back door and went around to the next house. Most of the furniture was there, but nothing else was, so he headed to the next place. The old timer cabin was backed up against the other side of the little valley. An even older looking shelter was mostly covered with dirt and grass. It looked to be built into the side of the hill.

The rusty knob broke off when he twisted it, so he pushed hard on the dilapidated door. One hinge broke off and the door swung in at an angle. He stepped in and found a very dusty table in the far corner to his right. Part of the back wall had caved in and left a mound a few feet high in the middle. In the left corner was an old metal cabinet with two doors that opened from the middle. He could hardly open the rusted doors but, when they started to move, they came open suddenly. He was disappointed when he found the shelves bare.

As he looked around, he could see something under the table, so he walked over to it. The light from the small window was barely enough to see much of anything, especially since the window was so dirty. The light coming in from the door helped, but the shelter was surprisingly deep. As he walked by the mound of dirt, he kicked something that immediately drew his attention. As he dug around, he discovered what appeared to be an old rusted milk crate. After he was able to pull it from the dirt, he found that there were nine canned jars of food of some sort inside. Five of them were rusted through on top and one was broke. He wiped off the remaining three jars with a watering mouth. One was meat of some sort, another looked like pears, and the last was a mixture of potatoes, carrots and meat stock. *What,* he thought, *no bread and butter*? Still, he was extremely surprised at his fortune. He returned to the house and immediately started filling his stomach. Lucky was more than happy to help him eat what they could.

As soon as he was finished eating the rush of blood to his stomach made him sleepy. He knew he had to keep moving, even though he only had enough food for one more meal. He dumped everything together into one jar and put on the best lid he had. He tucked the other two jars out of sight, and then went out the back door. He did not bother to lock it.

The trees on the hill were thicker, so the leaves they dropped made the incline slipperier. Dane did not want to have to go by all of the houses, but the moisture on the leaves decided for him.

He was feeling much better as he crept from one building to another. A paved road started up the slanting valley and disappeared into the trees. He kept Lucky at his side and sometimes held his collar before moving to the next house. He nearly fell as he tripped over something under a layer of leaves.

One more house and he would have to head out through the trees to the road. He crept up to the last house looking around for anything in particular when, suddenly, Lucky looked up and jumped back. Pain and a huge flash of light exploded in Dane's head as he fell to the ground unconscious.

CHAPTER 19
SUSAN

As a gangly, long legged, young girl with braces, Susan was picked on by the usual culprits. New to the area, she had been barely fitting in. She hung out with a few new friends, trying to blend in. Soon some name calling led to one bully cornering her. She could vividly remember his tousled red hair and too many freckles across his nose. Her friends were nowhere to be seen as the bully smacked her books out of her hands. The leering face suddenly rocketed backward and landed with a meaty thud. A slightly bigger boy now stood facing her where the other one was. There was no leer on his face, only a slight flushed look of anger. After picking up her books and handing them back to her, he turned and picked the trouble maker off the ground and began explaining the errors of his ways to him.

Susan had been at a loss why this boy, Chris, had singled her out as needing help. Others were picked on too, but this was the first time she had seen anyone stand up for someone else. As the newest student to the school, she was surprised at how friendly most of the small-town kids had been. All except the red headed kid, who slunk off with a mixture of embarrassment, anger, and pain on his face.

After that, the two of them became close friends. They were quite the sight together, since she was small, skinny with large glasses. He had been several inches and a good fifty pounds heavier than her. They lived several miles apart, but that did not stop them from finding ways to be together. He taught her how to ride a horse, shoot a rifle, and drive a stick shift. Once they were old enough and got their drivers licences, they were nearly inseparable.

On one of the few occasions that they were apart, Susan had been in another state for her grandfathers funeral. Her family had planned on staying several days, but she had come back early to take care of her sick horse. The next day after her arrival, her wonderful world turned upside down.

After the radioactive fallout, the wind and storms, the looting and killing, the loss of her dear horse, and worse, her home, she finally managed to get up to the summer cabin by the lake. Day after day she had waited for her parents to come. Dozens, if not hundreds, of others showed up, but there was not enough room for everybody, and even more people died. She had kept the doors locked and blocked off, so nobody could get inside. Her cozy little shack had enough supplies for several months, but she was desperate for word from her parents and Chris. She eventually took in another teen girl, even though it would severely cut into her food supply. She was somewhat relieved when the small town came together and picked a leader.

Her relief was short lived when the "Boss", the new leader who came along with his religious fervor about Mother Earth and all that bull, tried to "give" her to a fat, older guy. He had been pounding on her door for a few days before he backed off, and when a knock on her door made her almost put a bullet through the door to make him go away, she opened the door to find Chris there, looking happy and sad at the same time. It was then that she vowed never to let him out of her sight again.

Chapter 20
Decisions to Make

The "Boss" led Wayne and the rest of the bunch into his home. He quick-fired each of them questions. They hardly had time to answer before he fired off another one, sometimes on an entirely different subject. He was undoubtedly highly intelligent but seemed a bit off kilter. There was a strange mixture of religion, military, and something else he could not quite figure out. After the questions stopped, he regaled them with his vision of what the Commonwealth of San Isabel would be in the years ahead. The man firmly believed that they were the last people in the United States and that their offspring would repopulate the country. He announced that it was their parties' duty to Mother Earth to help them in their quest. He would not stop them if they wanted to leave, but their weapons would have to stay to protect the "Chosen Ones" from harm.

They all started to complain at once, but he merely stood up and put his arms out. "My children know not what they reap," he said in a sing-song voice. "The Blessed Mother has chosen only a few to repopulate her world, and we all have our roles to play. So I strongly suggest you stay," he said. He stood towering over them as he pointedly looked at Connie. He made a small bow and then said, "May the Blessed Mother be kind to you. You may go." He turned and walked down a narrow hallway and closed the door. The meeting was over.

As they stepped out of the motor home, a young lady was waiting for them. She had kind eyes but seemed tired. "Follow me," she said. "You may stay in any of these three homes." She pointed them out as they approached some run down looking travel trailers. "All of the good ones are taken, but you'll be warm at night. May The Mother be kind to you." She turned and went back to turning the soil in the empty garden, leaving the four people standing there.

"What the hell did we get ourselves into?" Frank asked. "That freak in there took our weapons!" He started pacing. Breathing deeply, he tried to calm down.

"Quiet down, Dad, there are people watching us. Lets go inside and talk about what we're going to do."

They filed into the largest of the travel trailers-about 25 feet long. It was well kept inside and had blankets and towels folded up and stacked up on the counter. There were cups, plates and silverware in their proper places. There was no food to be found. A quick check showed that they had running water.

Perra filled up some glasses of really cold water and passed them out. Wayne sat at the table waiting for everyone else to sit down. Before anyone started talking, he said very quietly, "We may be under surveillance, so don't say anything important."

They discussed the recent happenings and only mentioned tiny tidbits of information. They talked of their mission, which was no secret, and of what they wanted to do. Stay and contribute or head further south to find people. They actually had no plans to head south. That was merely a decoy in case they were allowed to leave.

Suddenly they could hear little kids' voices laughing and shouting, as kids do when they are cooped up inside for a long time. They all got up and went to the windows on the other side of the trailer and looked out. Several kids aged two to ten were coming out of one of the buildings. Three women came out with them, each with infants. The kids went straight for some toys, swing sets, and tricycles in an open shed next to their building. They were all taken back by the sight of such young kids.

Connie suddenly had an unpleasant feeling about the whole place. It was starting to look like a fanatic's breeding ground. She was still able to get pregnant and did not want any part being a "Chosen One". She could see what she would be "chosen" for.

Perra's face lit up at seeing the children running around and playing. A distant memory brought a pang of longing. She had been a preschool teacher for many years and truly missed their innocence and straightforwardness. Until she had seen the kids, she did not realize how much she missed them.

As Wayne surveyed the little ones outside, he wondered why there were no older children around. Now that he thought about it, he had seen a few teens, but none younger until now. There were none in between. He started to mention it when another group came out of another door on the opposite end of the same building. This group had several ranging from about ten to fourteen.

Wayne started to get the same feeling that Connie got.

Lucky for Perra, she had already started Menopause. He made eye contact with Connie, who looked stricken.

"I think we should continue our journey. This place looks as if they can do without us," he said loud enough for anyone spying on them.

"Agreed," Connie and her father said at the same time.

Perra looked yearningly at the kids, but after a few seconds said, "Ok honey ko, if that's what you want to do."

A few hours later they were still chatting while playing cards. They heard a knock on their door, so Frank got up to answer it. He found a very pregnant teenager standing there in a long dress that was tight across her stomach. She merely said, "Dinner will be served in that building over there in about fifteen minutes." She turned and pointed to a long rectangular building. She turned back and said with down-cast eyes, "May the Blessed Mother be kind to you," and headed off to get her meal.

They walked over together and got in a small line that went out the door. As they went in, a wonderful aroma of spiced meat and vegetables met them. There was a buffet table with baked bread, potatoes and corn, along with three large roasts. They filed down the line and dished up then found a place on one side of a long table.

Nobody was eating, so they sat in anticipation of a speech from their leader.

As the last person sat down, the Boss got up. He dressed in what looked like a priest's robe, a tall, flat topped hat with something painted on it, a cummerbund and a long gnarled staff with a crystal on the end. His resemblance to Merlin was comical.

He launched into a sing-song chant that praised the

Blessed Mother of All, and thanked Her for sparing them as the Chosen Ones. Under Her bountifulness they were the inheritors of the New World, and would be remembered in history as the progenitors of The Blessed Mother's New World Order. He went on to welcome the newcomers, and hoped they would find fulfillment as Children of Her teachings.

Most of the people were quite personable and asked them many questions. They avoided asking about the outside world, only about the newcomers themselves. Only a few looked upon them with a little suspicion, including Jose, who sat a few seats away from the Boss.

After dinner, everyone cleared their plates and took them up to a window, where a few young girls took them from them. They excused themselves and headed back to the trailer they had been using.

They sat and talked of the delightful meal and of the people they met. After a while, the cards were brought out again, and they played until it was too dark to see. They decided to turn in for the night, so Frank and Connie went out and over to the next camper trailer. Connie took the bed in back as her father stretched out on the one in front.

As Wayne and Perra went back to their bed, a silent figure rose from beside the trailer and crept into the darkness.

Chapter 21
Friend or Foe?

Dane's head felt like a ton of bricks got dropped on it. He groaned as he became aware of his surroundings. At first he could not figure out where he was, then thought that he must have been to one hell of a party the night before. He tried to sit up, but it made him nauseous, so he lay back down on the bed. *Bed*, he asked himself, *whose bed is this*? He turned his head to check out the room, and nearly vomited.

"Try not to move," said a female voice. "You have a nasty cut on your head. I thought you were dead, but my boyfriend said you'll be OK. Lucky for you, I know how to sew."

"What the hell happened?" Dane asked while painfully touching the sutures.

"You were sneaking around and set off one of our trip wires, so I clobbered you. We thought you were one of the "Chosen Ones", but after you were out, we didn't recognize you and brought you and your dog inside. He's very friendly, by the way."

Another figure walked in and looked at Dane. Seeing him upside down did not help his head any, so he closed his eyes.

The face looking at him did not look more than twenty. He felt intensely despondent knowing that a kid got the drop on him. "Who are you?" He managed.

"You aren't in a position to ask any questions," said the upside-down face. "The same applies to you, and why were you sneaking around this house?"

"Do you have anything for a huge hangover?" Dane asked, buying time.

"That's no hangover," the young man answered, not getting the pun. "I dropped a small sledge hammer on your head as you were standing under our window. You moved right at the last second, so you ended up with a nasty cut."

"We have some aspirin, but you still haven't answered my question," he continued.

Dane managed to swing his feet off the bed and sit up. His head still swam with pain, but he did not want to throw up anymore. "I'll tell you what, I'll answer any questions you have if I can have some of your aspirin."

The two captors looked at each other and nodded. The girl got up and left.

Dane sized up the young man standing in front of him. They were about the same height, but the stranger had him by a solid fifty pounds. He had familiar features to his face, but he could not quite place where he had seen them before.

The young woman came back in with a canteen, Dane's canteen, and handed it and some aspirin to him.

After gratefully swallowing them with plenty of cool water, Dane wiped at some that spilled down his chin. "Ok," he said. "My name is Dane. I was sneaking around this house because I was making my way up the valley, and didn't want to be seen."

The guy looked surprised at his frankness. "Why do you want to go up there? Do you know what kind of people are up there?" He asked with an intense look.

"My family was taken that way. I only know that they went with some strangers, semi-willingly. It was very strange. Do you know anything about them?"

"Only that they are a bunch of fanatics that'll rape and impregnate any woman capable of having a baby," interjected the girl fiercely. "Did you have any women over sixteen with you?"

"Yes, my girlfriend is thirty-nine and my sister-in-law is forty-nine, but she is post menopausal."

"Then we're going to have to get your girlfriend out of there as soon as possible. It won't be easy either. They've been building a huge fence around their village. I would not be surprised if they build in look-out areas and keep them armed," said the girls boyfriend.

"It sounds as if you've had a run in with them."

"Yes, we've had a run in with them several times. I had to break Susan out after they tried to pair her off with a slime ball guy named Jose. After that, we kept going back at night and taking whatever food we could pack out. A few weeks later, they moved up further into the hills. We kept getting away with fruit and vegetables until they put their campers, trailers and motor homes in a circle around the garden.

"Is Jose their leader?"

"No, his brother used to be, but disappeared while hunting. A creepy skinny guy that just goes by "Boss" runs it now, and Jose thinks *he* killed him," Susan said.

"Ever since the Boss took over, things are ran almost military style and nothing happens without him knowing about it."

Dane pondered the new information for a few seconds, and then said, "how far up the road are they?"

"It's about an hour hike from here. They come this way once a day, to trade out their lookout."

"Where do they get their gas?

"They make it in one of their sheds. It's ethanol, made from corn," the young man said. "That's why we were able to get a lot of corn. They grow loads of it."

"How many people live there, and how many weapons do they have," Dane asked more authoritatively.

Susan answered, "About sixty, with just under half being kids. There are only about twelve to fourteen men and about twenty adult women."

"And weapons?" Dane asked.

"They keep them in the back of a locked and armored truck. Before they brought it inside, we were able to get a few," added the guy.

"By the way," he said, "sorry for knocking you out. You already know Susan. My name is Chris." He held out his hand expectantly.

"Chris..." Dane had his hand half way up, but hesitated while the pieces fit together. "What's your mother's name?"

Chris' brows met as his hand slowly lowered. "Connie, why?"

Danes mind spun as he tried to organize his thoughts.

"Do you know my mother? Is she alive? Do you know where she is?"

"Yes," Dane said, "and you're not going to like it."

CHAPTER 22
A CHOSEN ONE

Frank woke up shortly after the sun came up. He had a hard time falling asleep, and when it finally came he slept fitfully. He had dreamt that shadows were following him and trying to steal something from him. He stretched while yawning and still under his blankets. He reached for his boots, but they were not where he remembered leaving them. Still groggy from sleep, he grabbed them and put them on. After lacing them up and putting on his shirt, he went back to the bedroom where his daughter slept.

"Rise and shine, beautiful," he said. He knocked on the folding partition. Getting no answer, he opened it up enough to look inside. He found only a messed up bed. Thinking she must have gotten up early he turned and went back to the front and went out into the chilly morning air. He walked up to the trailer Wayne and Perra stayed in and knocked on the door, then went inside. He was somewhat perplexed when he did not find her there, so he went back to the bedroom. Their partition was not closed, but he knocked before getting too close.

"Wayne, have you seen Connie?"

Wayne woke up quickly and rose up on his elbows. His hair did an excellent imitation of Buckwheat's hair as he lay there staring at Frank.

"No. I've been sleeping. Didn't she stay with…?" He suddenly threw off his blankets and pulled on his pants. "I knew we should have left yesterday," he said while shaking Perras shoulder.

After dressing they filed out of the trailer, only to face several armed men with the Boss standing in the middle of them. "You have no need to fear for the safety of Connie. She has been Chosen by Gaia, the Blessed Holy Mother."

"Like hell she has," Frank said furiously. He started walking toward the Boss but was stopped by Wayne's grip. "Let me go God damn it!" He tried to shake Wayne's hand off, but it held firm.

"Evidently you are of the Damned," said the self-appointed priest. God has spoken, and *She* does not want you here. Fortunately for you we no longer kill the Damned. Our Mother has forbidden me to kill any more people," he said with dull patience.

"She doesn't belong here with you *freaks*," Frank said with spittle flying.

The closest man near him stepped forward and struck him in the belly with the butt of his rifle, dropping Frank to his knees. "You will *not* speak of the Chosen Ones in that manner," said the priest. "Rest assured that Connie will be well-taken care of. Her offspring will help repopulate the world in Her Glory. You may now take your vehicle and leave. Mercy will not be shown upon you if you return.

Wayne's jaw muscles stood out. He kept a tight reign

on his anger. He blamed himself for their current situation. If he had not relaxed his guard, they would not be in this predicament. His helplessness was nearly overwhelming as he helped Frank to his feet.

Perra, who started to cry, grabbed Franks other arm and helped him walk over to the truck. They all climbed in the front and closed the doors. The keys were in the ignition, so Wayne started it up. He carefully backed up, then drove slowly in a circle and headed out the front entrance. The planks were laid down again. He fumed as he drove up to, and over, the ditch.

CHAPTER 23
A DANGEROUS MISSION

After popping some more pain pills, Dane was ready to go. He hardly slept that night and woke up early. His head still ached, but he could not wait around to get better.

Chris told him of the hundreds of people that the Chosen Ones had killed in the name of their religion. If they did not believe, or just could not fit in, they were killed. For some reason that he did not know about, they stopped killing a few months before. Maybe, he postulated, because they were running out of people for their gene pool.

They ate a light breakfast of stale corn bread and deer jerky, washed down with fresh spring water.

The road that led up to the main road was about a quarter of a mile long. They just made it passed the junction of the two roads when they heard a vehicle coming. All three of them quickly retreated, and flattened against the cold, wet grass on the sloping hillside. Dane sent the dog after a stick further down the hill. After a few seconds of laying there, Dane said, "Stay here." He quickly got up and stepped up on the side of the road.

Wayne almost did not see his brother appear on the side of the road as he drove down the twisting pavement. He immediately braked and came to a stop a dozen yards down the road.

Dane was not sure if his family was in the truck or not, so he had told the two to stay where they were. There was no sense in exposing them just yet. Seeing his brother jump out of the driver's seat sent a wave of relief through him.

"They've got Connie," Wayne said without preamble. "Frank has a sore gut, but otherwise we're okay."

"What happened to your head?" He asked Dane as he saw the bump and shaved off area on his head.

"I found Connie's son, Chris. Actually, he found me and dropped a sledge hammer on my head. I'll tell you about it later." He waved Chris and Susan over and made quick introductions.

"Chris? Is that you, son?" Frank asked. He got out of the truck and held him at arms length. "Damn, boy! You put on some weight!"

Chris was wordless as he looked at his grandfather. He had thought him long dead, along with his mother. His brows knotted together, "Grandpa? What... how... I thought you were dead." He held onto his grandfather's arms and looked back in astonishment. Before he could say anything more, he was in a fierce hug. He looked over his grandfather's head and looked at Susan with an embarrassed shine to his cheeks.

When Chris was finally able to breathe again, he had to sit down for a minute. First his mother had come back from the dead, and now his grandfather. It was all so unexpectedly overwhelming.

"Tell me what happened Chris." Frank was clearly worried

at his grandson's reaction. The kid turned white, then nearly passed out.

In a slight daze, Chris began telling his story.

"When I went home after Dad died, I found the note from Mom. I stayed for four or five days and waited, but she didn't come back from tracking the men that killed Dad. I assumed they got her too. I couldn't stay at the ranch alone, so I headed back out to try and find Susan."

His anguish was evident as he talked of his feelings of guilt.

"I wasn't there when Dad was killed, and felt like I could have stopped it. Then my promise to Susan kept me going out time after time." He shared a quick look at Susan, who was by his side with tears in her eyes. "I promised to protect her, and raise a house full of children together. After Mom disappeared I went in search of Susan, only to blow a hose on my radiator. At that point, I was half out of my mind with grief. My only remaining thought was to find Susan. I don't remember much of the trip from the highway to her house, even though it was several miles of walking. When I approached her parent's house and found it burned to the ground, I nearly lost it completely. Then I remembered that they had a small summer cottage up by the reservoir. I figured I would surely find her there. The trip up the road was almost too much for me. There were all kinds of burned out vehicles. Many had been pushed off the side of the road. The stench of rotting bodies made me dry heave several times. Once I made it through that, I eventually came to the ripped out road that went across the front of the reservoir. I remember sinking down on my knees and crying like a baby. I was ready to jump off the edge of the road when I saw smoke coming up from a chimney on the other side of the reservoir. With the last of my energy, I walked around the old lake and through the mud from the mountain. I had to slog a lot of mud and debris that had flowed down the mountain side."

Without realizing what was happening, Chris was guided into the back of the truck. His mind was still in shock as the truck headed down the road.

"After a few days of rest, I got invited to join their group. A much nicer man was in charge of the group. He had a vision of starting a new world, a new society without the tyranny of a large government. One that was much simpler, and would obey the needs of the people, instead of the needs of the few. I was impressed, and immediately agreed."

"Within a few hours of joining the group, I found out Susan. She had been living in their cottage with another single woman."

He chuckled, then said "I thought she was going to faint when she saw me in the doorway. I settled right in, and the other woman found another place to stay."

"A few weeks later we heard about our leader's demise. They said he was killed in a hunting accident. The new leader stepped in so smoothly that no one seemed to think much about it. The old leader's brother made a fuss about the "accident" but was paid off by the new boss. The payment, to make him shut up, was for him to be paired with his choice of women in the group. His choice was Susan. She was thin and athletic, not to mention good looking. Ever since I got there, I'd seen him staring at her. I was pissed off and confronted the new boss, as well as Jose. I got an earful of some religious bullshit. Before I knew it, I flattened Jose and got in a glancing punch to the face of the skinny bastard that had given Susan away. The cut to my knuckle was nothing compared to the gratification of seeing his broken front tooth. I took off, but before I escaped I tried to find Susan. She was nowhere to be found, and our place was messed up like a fight had broken out inside. I almost made it out of town before someone took a shot at me."

"A few days later I was able to find, then sneak Susan out. When Jose found out about it, he was really pissed off. He hunted us for several days afterwards, but I grew up hunting these hills. I know not only *where* to hide, but how. I only left a trail when I wanted to."

A bump in the road brought Chris back to reality. Susan had her arm around his shoulders and looked concerned. Her fiancé had been through too much, and she was terrified of him losing his mind. When the glaze in his eyes was replaced by anger, she knew he was going to be okay.

"Amazing," Frank said.

"Now what about Mom?" He suddenly realized they were heading down the winding road.

"We have to go back and get her," Chris said loudly. He brooded for several seconds before his anger got the better of him. "Where are you going? We are going the wrong way," he said sternly.

"We can't go back yet," his grandfather said. He had been sitting across from Chris and had been watching the boy closely. "I'm sure they're expecting us to try to come back for her. Right now we only have three weapons; yours, Susan's and Danes. We are out-gunned and out manned. We have to bide our time and come up with a plan. We can't just go barging in there. Even with the protection of this truck, they'd kill us all.

Chris just sat and thought about it for a minute, looking for a way to refute his grandfather's words. When he could not think of anything, he looked him in the eye and nodded his acquiescence.

Wayne drove while furiously thinking about how to get Connie back. He ticked off the obstacles in his head; The fortress was too solid to try to punch through. To burn it down was unthinkable, since there were too many innocents that could be hurt. The open trench would be too slow to cover and drive through, find her, then get out again. Finding her would be the main problem once they managed to get in, but how? His mind ground on as he carefully drove down the winding road.

Dane was dangerously quiet while he sat beside his brother. He was running tactical scenarios in his head and kept coming up with disaster any way he looked at it. Anything short of digging under the walls came out bad. They would have to go all the way back to their home and re-arm. Even then, they would be out numbered. Their only chance would be to use quiet weapons and stealth. His mind awhirl, he saw nothing as they headed away from his lady.

Perra was terribly sad and could not help but cry for her friend. The first lady friend she had in two years had been taken away, and already missed her. She could feel the anger and frustration emanating from the others in the back of the truck. To keep herself busy, she started looking through their meager supplies for something for everyone to eat.

Wayne pulled into the small town that they made the mistake in the last time. This time he went all the way through and up to the grown-over mudslide. He stopped the truck, turned off the engine and got in the back. Dane came in a few seconds later. It was a little cramped with six of them, the dog, and their few supplies. What he had to say would only take a few minutes anyway.

"We have to go back to the shelter. We don't stand a chance against them with just three rifles. If we hurry, we can be back by nightfall. I don't think they will expect us to be back so soon. So just *maybe*, we can surprise them."

"They will have sentries out," Dane said. "There's also a lookout in the diner that we stopped at before. I just saw him as we went passed. We need to figure out how to come from an unexpected direction. Chris, you told me that you got Susan out of their camp. How did you do it?"

All heads turned to Chris as he looked at Susan. "I had help. I know one of the ladies in their camp that was sympathetic to us. She used to be the librarian at my high school. She came to me offering to help when they took Susan away from me. She won't be able to help this time. They were still here in town and had not moved to the new site. The last time I was out there they were just starting to build the walls around the camp. She used to put out some food for us to eat," he added.

"What time did you go on your food raids before they moved?"

"I went between three and four in the morning. That seems to be the best time."

Frank was standing at the back of the truck with his binoculars up. "We are under surveillance. I suggest we get out of sight before anyone shows up."

"You're right Frank," Dane said. Wayne nodded his agreement. "We should have known about the lookout, and kept going."

The two brothers got out of the back and quickly got in the front, started the truck and headed across the bumpy pathway leading around the empty lake.

The going was just as slow as it was the first time, but they were too preoccupied with their own thoughts to think about the uncomfortable ride. When they came to the log they built up with dirt, Wayne just went right over it without stopping. He kept going when he hit the paved road and only slowed when he came to the smaller mudslide. Without paying much attention to them, he continued passed the burned out vehicles and headed down the mountain. Before he knew it, he was turning into a grassy field sprinkled with autumn ripened trees and evergreens.

They hardly said anything as they headed inside their home. Dane, Wayne, and Frank went immediately to the weapons and started grabbing what they could carry.

Chris and Susan were in awe of the hidden shelter as Perra gave them a quick tour. Since they were all hungry, the women went upstairs and prepared a quick meal, along with a few more days supplies just in case they had to stay longer.

As they all sat down to eat, Dane spoke first. "I think we need to come down the road from the other direction. If I were them, I'd be setting up traps and lookouts all along the way we went. I'd probably even send people out the opposite direction just to be safe."

"The Boss is very intelligent," Chris said, "but he doesn't have any military experience. I heard rumors that he was a political art's professor, before he got fired for sexual harassment. I'm pretty sure a few of the guys he has with him were in the military. From what I've been able to hear, the idea of the wall was from one of them."

"Do you know of any roads that can take us to the other side of their fortress," Wayne asked.

"Yes, there are dirt roads that go all over the hills and plains. It's been a long time since I've been on them, and hopefully they are still useable, but I'm sure I can get us to the other side."

"Ok, so after we get there what are we going to do," Frank asked. "There's only one way in and out of that place.

"I think a distraction is in order. After we get them checking out one area, we'll walk in the front and get Connie. It will be a mad house with everyone wanting to see what's going on," Dane said.

"Only a few should go in," Wayne added. If we all show up, it's more likely that we will be noticed. He turned to Chris. "How many people know your face there?"

"About a half dozen, I didn't stick around very long," he said, looking at Susan.

"I am a total stranger to them," Dane said. "I'm not sure if it's best for me to go, or use someone that they've seen before. They might remember your face, but be too busy to realize who you are. They might remember and go after you. What do you all think?"

"I'll go," Wayne said immediately. Besides Chris, I'm the only other one in decent shape. If we have to, we can run. I know Connie is still in good shape."

For the next forty minutes, they hashed out their plan. They figured their route to the other side of the encampment and possible ambush points. When they were done, Frank and Wayne went downstairs and started putting the "distraction" together.

"What about Lucky?" Perra asked.

After a brief pause, Dane said, "We should take him. If we leave him and don't come back, he'll die of dehydration. We might need him if anyone tries to sneak up on us."

They all dressed in either camouflage clothes, or whatever

they had that was dark. Perra gathered the charcoal from the small stove, so they could use it to darken their skin, and also to keep the sheen on their faces down.

They were soon loaded and headed back to Connie's ranch. They needed to refill the propane tank on the truck and get a few more supplies.

Chris drove the truck this time since he knew the back roads. He had a somewhat difficult time adjusting to the old truck since it had a lot more weight and the viewing ports were small.

A few of the roads were almost grown over and in several places had been almost washed out beyond use, but he managed to get them to the black top on the other side of their goal.

It took them nearly four hours to get passed all of the obstacles, and still had a few hours of daylight before they would be ready. They would need to wait until early morning before they sprang their surprise.

As they made their way up to the paved road, everyone that had binoculars watched for anything suspicious. Being jostled around in the back of the truck resulted in a black eye for Frank. He took it stoically, since he would go through hell to get his daughter back.

Chris took his time once he got to the black top. He soon stopped and let Wayne take over. "Their camp is down the road a few miles," he said, relieved that he did not have to drive any longer. His back was cramped from having to bend down to see out the slats over the window.

Wayne turned right, pulled off the main road, and onto a promising dirt road that went into the low hills. He looked for a place to lay low for the next several hours, and soon found what he was looking for. There were a few other houses within sight of the dwelling he pulled up beside.

Chris kicked in the side door to the garage, then unlocked and lifted the tall garage door. Wayne backed in and shut the engine down as everyone unloaded.

They were all stiff from the bumpy ride and tired from the long, emotional day. They headed into the long abandoned house and looked around. It was in moderately good condition. In the laundry room, one of the back windows was broken out, due to a fallen tree branch. The rest of the house was clean and dry.

"Remember," Wayne said to everyone, "no fire and no light after dark. Stay away from the windows, and don't do *any*thing that would indicate that we are here."

Chris helped unload the food and a few other supplies. Perra set up the portable white gas stove and started heating up their main dish of canned elk. Everything else would be eaten cold.

After eating they sat down in the large living room and went over their plan again and then again. It was critical to have the timing down. All of them that still had working watches reset them together. After chatting for a half hour, most of them went to find a place to get some sleep. Dane was too wound up to sleep, so he kept watch. He soon had Chris by his side as they quietly chatted and kept watch together.

After a while, Dane left Chris on watch and went out to the garage with some masking tape. He taped up the back lights as best he could. Then he went to the front lights and totally covered the left light. On the right headlight, he covered up most of it, and left a few inches clear. He found a screwdriver on the wall and adjusted the light so that it pointed more to the right. He wanted to be able to see the side of the road just enough to keep from going off it. If anyone followed them, at least there would be minimal light for them to see. He grinned, thinking of the surprises soon coming their foes way. As soon as he completed the front lights he got in the cab of the truck and took out the light bulb. He needed his night vision now more than anything.

At 2 AM their watch alarms went off simultaneously. Perra was already up and had hot coffee ready. They quickly prepared for their assault on the compound.

By 2:15 AM they all had their face and hands smeared with charcoal, and were soon on their way. Dane drove down the road slowly as his eyes adjusted to the dark. What light came from the lone headlight was barely enough to see. When he got to the paved road, he stopped. Chris jumped out and placed a few hand sized rocks on the other side of the pavement. They were markers for the turn off about a mile ahead.

With his heart racing in anticipation, he jumped back in as Dane took off.

At about a mile from the compound Dane shut the lights and engine off, then coasted to a stop. The early morning fall had a wintery bite to it, and the stars looked unusually bright. A half moon provided just enough light to see the road ahead. Even with the binoculars, it was extremely hard to see anything, much less into the shadows of the trees. Anyone could be waiting for them as they looked into the trees.

Wayne got up on top of the roof of the cab. He would be the extra eyes for the next half mile. He barely felt the cold as he peered into the night. The truck quietly crept up the road. Just before the compound came into sight, Dane pulled over. They all watched carefully for the next several minutes for any movement.

Wayne, Chris, Dane and Susan armed themselves and

grabbed a few packages made up several hours before. They headed into the tree line and headed for the compound. After several minutes of stealthily making their way through the trees, they came near the end of the tree line. There was about 20 to 30 feet of bare land between the trees and the solid wall of logs. Dane scouted the area but could not see any tracks in the light frost on the ground. That was a good sign. If they had sentries walking the exterior, it would slow him down. He went back into the trees, and they continued around the compound. They went as far as the trees could take them, and then stealthily made their way to the wall. They continued on until they could see the unfinished opening. The heavy boards to cross the trench were nowhere to be seen. Checking his watch, Dane waved the others down. They still had a several minutes until it was time.

Dane and Chris left the others behind and crept up to the opening. Trained in jungle warfare and other various conditions, Dane was the first to see the trip wire. He grabbed Chris and kept him from setting it off. It was poorly set up. Dane felt better knowing he was not up against professionals.

A small travel trailer was on the other side of the opening. Dane did not remember it being there. *It was probably dragged there as a guard shack*, he thought. Try as he might, he couldn't see anyone inside.

Wayne and Susan came up to the others with a wave from Dane. They all quietly huddled near several logs that were in various stages of preparation for use on the wall. With pulses pounding and various scenarios playing out in their heads, they waited for the signal. When it came, they could not miss it.

With a few minutes to go, they all un-slung their weapons. Dane strained as he loaded the cross bow, then gave it to

Susan. He took a package from his back pack and got it ready. Susan, who grew up knowing how to use a rifle, quietly took the crossbow. She set it aside and quickly readied a similar package.

On the other side of the compound, Frank placed a three-gallon propane tank on the wall. He could barely see between the poles, and hoped it was opposite of where the front of the motor home was. He placed another one at the back of where the motor home should be. From their earlier trip inside the compound, they saw that the Boss's home had vehicles in open make shift carports on either end. If they could take him out along with the vehicles, nobody could follow them. He made sure to attach the tanks high enough to take full advantage of the gaps between the trees.

Perra, on the same side as Frank, was nervously holding a bow with an arrow ready. She hardly knew how to hold the thing, much less shoot it. Regardless, she stood her ground, searching for anyone coming around the perimeter.

Lucky looked out of the front of the cab, confused by the strange behavior of his people.

Frank checked his watch to make sure he got the timing right. He took a deep breath and expelled it quietly. It was almost time. Then, he quickly lit the newspaper sticking out of the package taped to the side of the propane bottle, then ran over to the other one and lit it. Then he ran like hell to the truck parked part way around the side of the compound. He drove as quietly as he could toward the opening.

At the scheduled time a large flash, then boom, shook the night, and then another. After a long twenty seconds, Wayne and Chris stepped across the ditch and casually walked around the wall and to the left. Wayne kept his rifle slung close to his body. They headed to the nearest camper and went between it and the wall. There was a space of several feet behind the ring of vehicles and campers. It was very dark, but they quickly made their way to the make-shift building where Susan said the women stayed. She also had a map from the woman that had left them food. She had drawn a simple lay out of the camp, complete with who stayed where.

In the main area, people were yelling and running toward the fireball that had awakened them.

Dane gingerly stepped down into the trench, then Susan jumped down. They spread out, and quickly readied their packages. Once Susan had hers placed, she peered up over the trench. She could see the sentry come out of the trailer just inside the right side of the opening. He had a rifle and seemed to be looking at where the other two guys went. He raised his rifle and started walking across the opening. As soon as Susan recognized the slimy bastard, she brought up the cross bow. She aimed carefully, since she would only have one shot.

Jose had his chair leaning against the wall when the boom awakened him. He had fallen asleep again but did not really care. He cleared his head and got up to go outside. He saw two men walking into the compound, heading behind the campers. He quickly realized who they were and headed out to deal with them. He quickly lifted his rifle, but paused when he saw a reflection to his left, near the trench. Turning to see what it was, he got a brief glimpse of something coming up at him. He barely had time to flinch when an arrow entered his throat and lodged in his brain stem. He died before he hit the ground.

Nearly all of the men, women and older children had come outside to see the fire that was engulfing the far end of the compound.

Wayne and Chris ran to the side of the building were they hoped to find Connie. They quickly entered the side door and went from door to door checking for her. The barracks style building had many small rooms with only a single bed. Most of the doors were left open as the occupants ran out. In the middle of the long building was an open area that held couches and play areas for the kids. They headed to the other side of the room, where they could see more bedrooms. An elderly woman stopped them in their tracks. "She's not here," she said. She had expected something from the serious-looking people that had been there earlier the day before.

"Where is she?" Chris asked desperately. He recognized her as the librarian that helped them in the past.

She gathered her heavy robe around her, "Follow me."

They exited the same door that they came in and went back along the dark alley way. "Those sons of bitches have gone too far," she said with disgust. In a few seconds, they came to an old silver trailer. There were bars attached to the large window on the front of the trailer. Chris had so much adrenalin pumping into his system that he grabbed one and ripped it off. Two-inch screws dangled from each end. Another came off just as easily. After the next one, his mother's face appeared. She appeared shocked to see her son alive, and just outside of her cell.

After her family and friends had been forced out the day before, she went into a deep depression. She feared they would do something stupid, like try to rescue her. She refused to eat, or to acknowledge her captors. They figured she would appreciate the niceties of companionship, heat, water and food after a few days of being locked up without it. What they did not know was that she had spent months alone, and she did not care at that point if she lived or died.

"Stand back," said Chris. He violently pulled another bar off. He swung the bar in his hands and smashed the three-by- four-foot window. Connie immediately climbed out the window. Chris held her tightly, but only for a second.

"Let's go," commanded Wayne.

"Let me come with you," pleaded the older lady.

Wasting no time, Wayne nodded and started to run. She would have to keep up.

They all ran the fifty yards back to the exit and continued around to the other side. They barely noticed the body lying in the dirt.

One of the men that was loyal to the Boss figured out early what was going on. He ran to the armory to get a weapon, but the guard disappeared. Desperate for a weapon, he found a large rock and started smashing the lock.

The guard ran over to see if the Boss was okay. Before he reached him, he saw someone run up to the armory. The man was in the shadows and was trying to break into the weapons truck. He quickly dropped to one knee and took a shot. The man in the shadow dropped like a rock.

Someone managed to get one of the trucks away from the blaze before it burned. All of the other trucks and the Boss's home were engulfed in smokey flames. As the guy was backing out, he saw some people heading out the front of the compound. He waved a few others over and yelled for them to get in the back.

Dane saw the truck coming and quickly lit his package, then signaled for Susan to do the same. They jumped out of the ditch and ran around the side where the truck was waiting for them.

The armory guard saw the truck heading toward the trench, and watched for anyone else to show themselves.

Frank drove the truck to the others on the other side of the still-unfinished entryway. After they quickly loaded in, he punched the accelerator. He was still turning around when the two smaller propane and gun powder bombs went off, caving in the trench.

The fireballs caused the man driving the truck to slam on the brakes, sending a few of the men in back to the hard ground.

Frank could feel the heat through the small window and was glad that they built it the way they did. He could hear pieces of dirt and debris hitting the side of the truck. He was temporarily blinded from the flash, but the area was wide open and he knew somewhat where he was pointed. Several seconds later he gunned the engine, since he was better able to see. He stomped on the floor button for the brights and took off like a bat out of hell.

For the men and women that had seen the explosion in front, all they could see was a truck that was there one second, then it disappeared behind the wall of flame and dirt.

CHAPTER 24
THE ESCAPE

Frank slowed down after a few miles, because the road was not as straight up ahead. He kept nervously checking his side mirrors for any pursuit, but there did not seem to be any. The blow they dealt to the compound was immense, and probably left them in mass confusion. He hoped like hell that they took out the Boss. After a quick check, everyone seemed to be okay.

He did not think they needed to stop off at the house they stayed at earlier, so he kept going, passed the rocks on the side of the road. Once he turned off the main road and onto the dirt road he stopped and took the tape off the front lights. The road was bad in places, and he needed all the light he could get. He knew he probably did not have much time before they came after them. If any sentries were watching for them going the other way, it would not take them long to figure out where they went. The tracks going down the dirt road would be easy to follow.

With a sudden insight, he stopped. He stepped out of

the truck and onto the slightly frosty road. After explaining to the others and showing them the tracks behind the truck, they quickly had a make shift broom behind each back tire. It was not perfect, but it would make it harder for them to be followed. Each tree branch would have to be occasionally traded out for a fresh one. *Duct tape*, he thought as he got back behind the wheel, *you gotta love it.*

The eastern sky was starting to brighten as they drove into the early morning twilight.

Many of the obstacles they faced on the way out were the washed out roads. They seemed much worse as they were making their way back.

Shadows seemed to move in Franks peripheral vision, and was just too tired now that the adrenaline was gone. He got extremely sleepy and failed to slow down at one of the washed out places in the road. It registered just before he hit the washboard dip. The front bumper hit the soft dirt and dug in. The momentum of the truck pushed them through it. The people in the back had been sleeping the best that they could, and suddenly awoke when they were thrown into the air. Dane and Susan suddenly felt a crush of bodies on them. Everyone else had a somewhat softer landing.

Frank was immediately awake. He shut down the engine and jumped out to check on his passengers.

Someone was moaning when he opened the back door. All he saw was a jumble of bodies on and around the propane tank near the front of the bed. He climbed in and started helping the others up.

It was very dark inside, so he felt around until he found a hand. Someone turned on a flashlight, and he found himself looking at an attractive middle-aged lady. He had been introduced through the small window in the cab, but did not have the chance to see her until now. "Are you okay June?" She merely nodded. He gently helped her off somebody, and helped her sit down. He quickly went to the next person.

"What happened?" Chris asked.

"I hit a ditch. I just got too sleepy. I'm really sorry." Franks craggy face could not have looked more sad at the injuries he had caused.

"It's been a very long day, Frank. Don't blame yourself," said Wayne.

Connie was okay but slightly bruised. Wayne had a cut on the back of his head from someone's weapon. Chris was shaken but okay.

When he saw Dane, he knew he was hurt. Dane was pale and had a slightly glazed look to his eyes. After gently trying to help him sit up, Dane moaned again. "My arm," he managed to say.

Testing his arm with experienced fingers, Frank could find no compound break, much to his relief. He had raised many animals in the grasslands of his farm. Prairie dog holes caused him to lose more than a few animals. Still probing, he guessed that he had a fracture.

Susan got up without help but had a split lip.

Lucky had been asleep by the back door and had yipped at the sudden stop but was otherwise okay.

Perra was dead asleep in the front with her seat belt tight. After the crash, she had the sense to grab the first-aid kit in the glove box. As she saw each injury, she immediately started taking care of them. When she saw Dane, the only thing she could do was wrap his arm in a compression bandage and give him some pain pills.

After everyone was up and taken care of, Frank, Wayne, Connie and Chris went out to assess the damage to the front of the truck.

Their worst fears were confirmed even before they rounded the old truck. Radiator fluid was still running down the dry dirt gulch.

Connie was the first to see the splintered wood sticking out of the radiator. Her face was as sad as her fathers. Her husband had bought her the truck for their second anniversary. It was clear that they would not be driving the truck any further.

Except for Dane, everyone gathered around the battered front of the truck and contemplated their fate. Wayne soon snapped out of it. He turned to Chris and asked, "How much further do you think we have to go?"

Looking around in the gathering light, he said, "two, maybe three miles."

"We need to get moving. I know everyone is tired, but the Boss' thugs could show up at any time now."

"Before we head out," Connie chimed in, "let's at least push this out of the wash. I'd hate to come back and have to dig her out of the mud and debris."

They all helped push the truck out of the area, then quickly gathered what they could and headed down the road. They hardly looked back as they headed home.

"We'll find another radiator," said Frank while walking beside his daughter. She flashed him a small smile but said nothing.

CHAPTER 25
THE LIBRARIAN

June had been *so* close to retirement when it happened. She lost her husband a few years before, and had been planning on moving somewhere warmer, maybe Mexico. Along with her plans of retiring, she also lost her home and all of the many mementos she and her husband of nearly forty years had accumulated. All of the pictures, post cards, knick-knacks, antiques, and even her house were nothing but burned and washed away memories.

She had hunkered down in the basement with a few months supply of food, water, candles and flashlights. The radio was useless, the EMP ensuring it would never work again.

School hood memories of bomb drills had led her to books of World War II. The pictures and experiences of the survivors of Hiroshima and Nagasaki gave her a much clearer image of a nuclear war than most fictitious television shows ever could. So with visions of devastated landscapes and fried bodies, she had stayed in her basement, afraid to go outside. She ignored the knocking of her neighbors and stayed put, content to read from her eclectic collection of several thousand books.

A few days after the initial catastrophe, daylight had noticeably diminished. She finally went outside to see the effects first hand, and wished she had not. Almost everything had a light covering of fine ash, more than likely it was slightly radio-active.

The winds had picked up as the light decreased. Then the real barrage began. Lightning storms lit the land like she had never before experienced. Icy cold rain drops heavy with ash pounded down on the landscape, obliterating the view from her basement window. The fury outside shook the house and threatened to rip it from its foundation. Debris flew passed almost horizontally. In the first few hours, many roofs lost shingles. As the storm grew, whole roofs came off, with walls slamming down seconds later. Smaller buildings sheared off their foundations and rolled away before disintegrating into thousands of pieces. People that did not have basements, and many that did died a violent death. Week after week, the storm continued.

Born of the cold war, her house had a reinforced shelter in the basement. When her roof finally blew off, she had been in the shelter with the door secured. Boxes of books lined the concrete walls and helped keep in what little heat there was. June almost panicked when the roof of her shelter cracked from the shock of her two story home collapsing upon it. Part of her wanted to flee to the escape hatch. She knew that if she used the hydraulic lever to open the steel door, she would play hell getting it closed again, not to mention the water and debris flooding into her shelter.

After several more days, the rain stopped. The wind kept

up its howl, and made sleeping nearly impossible. Along with the constant dark, the cold kept nipping at her old extremities. Depression and anxiety loomed like giant teeth, ready to strike from behind. The one thing that kept her grounded, kept her sane, was her library. Every book she had ever bought, she kept. Years of garage sales, traveling and book clubs brought her collection to over thirty thousand. Some were rare and valuable, others common and well used.

Several days after the rains stopped, the wind finally slowed down enough for June to come out and survey the damage. Only houses of the sturdiest construction were still standing. Many of the taller trees were broke in half, or if not fallen over, tilted at assorted angles. Branches, insulation, clothing, glass, and construction materials blanketed the area. Broken trees stacked up on one side with a conglomeration of debris.

She had seen a few other survivors out wandering around, apparently still in shock. One old timer had a stubby cigar clutched in his teeth. He did not talk to her, and stumbled off up wind seemingly in search of something. What June did not realize was that, in a matter of minutes, the whole place would be burning. The old timer had tripped and dropped his stogey. The wind quickly blew the ember into a raging fire that headed right through the heart of the old neighborhood. As soon as she smelled the smoke, she headed for the basement shelter. She barely secured the door before the inferno started licking at her flattened walls. Smoke filtered in through the small vent high in the wall and caused her to cough. With burning eyes, she had to wrap a moistened towel around her face.

For nearly an hour, she waited for the inferno to burn itself out, then she stepped out through the fire rated door and up several concrete step to an alien landscape. Fire still engulfed the bigger trees and much of the area still smouldered. With a blanket wrapped around her, she walked out far enough to survey the heap that had been her home. As she had stood there surveying the devastation, a loud crack came from the other side of the remains of her house, and nearly scared her to death. One of the tall trees was still on fire. It burned through far enough to bring it down. When it did, it was on top of the of her only remaining purpose in life; her shelter. Debris, hot ashes and dust blew into her face and hair as she tripped and fell down. She quickly got up, brushing embers from her hair and clothes, burning her hands as she did so.

She stood frozen as burning rubble tumbled into her sanctuary, quickly igniting her books, pictures and the few other mementos she had time to squirrel away. She stood there without tears, without emotions, just there. At that point, she turned and walked down the ash and debris strewn street. The next thing she could remember was of standing outside the school library. It too, was burning.

Her memories of the next few days were a blur as she later tried to recall it. What she could remember was of a woman's haggard but friendly face, of a motor home and some driving. They had headed up into the hills, just before the wintery storms closed the roads. She remembered the small A-frame house, built of two by sixes, and with a green metal roof.

A few weeks later the built up pressure had finally broken free. She had helped clean up after a meal when she looked over at a picture on the wall. It was of an older couple at some scenic area with lots of evergreen trees stretching far behind them. She almost felt as if it were her and her husband, on one of their many trips, causing her throat to catch. She let out a moan and ran for the door. The swirling snow had piled up against it, causing her to falter. Two sets of hands pulled her from the frigid accumulation and cleaned her off. They wrapped her in a blanket and led her to her small room. As she sat on the bed, the tears would not stop, could not stop. The helplessness and sense of loss was overwhelming. Her new found friends held her close and accepted her return to sanity.

The next several months had seemed non-existent, and quickly led to a short spring and cool summer. People from all over the small mountain town had come together and pooled their resources.

By the next summer, they had come under the rule of a bizarre and scary leader, but many of them followed him for lack of any other leadership. The one good leader they did have, ended up dying in an accident. She knew better of course. She was used to studying people, and the body language of their new leader and his closest supporters told another story. She kept it to herself and only did what they asked of her. Even so, things quickly worsened. The Boss, as he wanted to be called, had a run in with a brazen young kid she recognized from her library. He had almost never been without his girlfriend, a thin, blonde girl. They, she knew, were good people. When the boy had mysteriously appeared out of nowhere, he was a sad and miserable young man. When he found his girlfriend, The change that had overcome him was amazing. That did not last, however. Several days later he had a confrontation with the Boss that lead to his running away. They had hunted him for a while, but to no avail. The girl disappeared a short time later. When food started disappearing, June knew who it was. Just before they were all forced to leave the area, she started sneaking some food out for them. She continued to do so until the wall was mostly done. After that, it was too risky to continue.

CHAPTER 26
THE CHASE

The Boss had sent the teenager he had been bedding back to her own room a few hours before. He was tall and lanky and liked his bed space. He woke up with a full bladder, and went into the small bathroom to relieve himself. Suddenly two quick explosions rocked his home.

"What the..." he cried as the concussion threw him against the wall. Confused, he got up and immediately staggered towards the exit several feet behind the passenger seat. Shaken and wobbly, he managed to get clear of his home before it went up in flames. His nose and one ear was bleeding, along with several smaller cuts on his body. He staggered several feet away before he collapsed.

The men and women closest to the Boss' place were the first to arrive and pull him away from the inferno. The chaos died down soon after the last bombs went off, and people started concentrating on putting the fire out. They came together with whatever they could find and formed a bucket brigade. One person manned the manual water pump until he got tired, and then joined the line as someone else took over. The kids that were strong enough to pass a bucket helped, the others got hustled back to their beds.

The men that had tried to go after the others picked up the two that had fallen, and made sure they were okay. They started hastily filling in dirt, so they could follow the intruders and take revenge. Before they finished, the man in charge of the armory unlocked and carried out weapons and ammunition to the rest of them. Opening the door, he realized that the man he shot was one of his own. He told the men shoveling that the invaders had shot their friend.

The initial blasts had only managed to create two small holes in the tough wood wall, but the propane had blown through the holes and all over both ends of the motor home. It also did an excellent job of igniting the dry timber with a force that was hard to reckon with.

The acrid smoke from the large motor home almost blotted out the moon as men, and a few women, used plywood shields to get close enough to throw water on it.

Once they were sure the fire was out on the motor home, they started working on the shed at one end. There was no hope for the vehicles inside. Once that shed was out, they moved to the other one, then on to the two holes and the fire blazing through them. They had no way to get out of the compound with buckets unless they walked, and worked instead on putting out the fire. Once the dirt got filled back into the large trench, they would be able to drive back and forth with water.

Most of the men filling in the dirt wanted to go after the people responsible for the destruction and the killing of the men. Others with calmer minds, wanted to fill the back of their only remaining truck with buckets of water and drive out to put the fire out, before it burned more of their wall and caused it to fall on their homes and buildings.

Within twenty minutes, there was enough dirt filled in and stomped down for the truck to make it through without getting stuck. They made several trips to put out the fire, and by then the Boss was on his feet and ready to kill. He quickly chose five men, loaded up and went after the people responsible. They turned down the road toward the old reservoir, but the lookout said nobody had come his way. They reversed their direction and sped off into the gathering light.

The Boss, previously known as Ken Halstead, fumed. *How dare they consecrate our sanctuary !? By the Mothers avenging anger, they will pay!*

At thirty-nine, he had spent many of his years shunned and turned out by the previous society. His fall from his prominent position had been the icing on the cake. He had enough of people and especially that tramp that practically threw herself at him, only to complain about his natural reaction to her youth and beauty.

He had gotten away from everything in his motor home only a few days before things went to hell. He simply loaded up and drove to the mountains. He had already been on the edge, but the destruction that followed his retreat from humanity seemed like a sign. The more he thought about it, the more he began to believe that he had been allowed to survive, that he was chosen to live. The more he pondered the more he became convinced that he was a Chosen One and that he must lead others to the light. Mother Earth allowed him to see what he must do, and to lead a small band of Chosen Ones, without destroying, maiming, polluting or restricting nature. He would repopulate the world in Her name, with reverence to nature.

Now, consumed with hatred and revenge, his knuckles were white. He focused with all of his energy as he sped up the winding road.

Every time he came to a road he stopped to see if the others had gone that way. Many of the roads had dirt, trees, tree limbs, and leaves on them and would show if anyone went that way. It was time consuming, but his need for revenge made him press on with an iron will. After many stops and starts, the Boss saw tracks going up a dirt road and into some low hills to the left. He stopped by the tire marks to discuss their find. They figured out that the others had gone in and back out again. The tracks nearest the paved road clearly showed them entering the area, then showed them leaving and heading towards his compound.

He was running out of options, since there were only a few more useable roads leading off the main road. Further up the hill, there was a large blockage that covered the road. The massive storms had eroded the dirt on the hillside where a castle had been built. The resulting mess was impassible with any wheeled vehicle.

One of the three men in front, an older teen named Tony, was the first to spot where their foes had disappeared. There were two sets of tracks leading into the mountains back and off to the right. The men whooped and hollered when they saw the tracks.

The Boss loudly cussed every time they crossed a washed out area of the road. The truck was a four cylinder pickup, and the extra weight caused them to scrape the bottom of the truck. The men in the back had to climb out until they made it to the other side.

When they saw the truck sitting on the side of the road,

the Boss' eyes became even more dangerous. He stopped a long way back. The area had undulating hills with lots of short evergreen trees. It was a prime area for an ambush, and he was not going to take any chances. With weapons loaded and ready, he sent a few men out. They stealthily approached, moving from tree to tree, until they got close to the vehicle. A few of them wanted to blast it, but the Boss wanted to be able to capture the Unfit, and take the truck back as a trophy, especially since he was driving their only useable truck.

"Come out or we will fill your truck full of holes," announced one of the men.

Yell as he did, nobody showed their faces, so he made his way safely up to the truck. His heart was racing as he reached it without getting shot. A quick peek into one of the small slots showed that nobody was home. He yelled to the others that it was empty. Once they all got closer and saw why it was still there, they briefly celebrated. Their prey was now on foot.

CHAPTER 27
TAKE COVER

Dane's leg was hurting again. He did his best to keep up with the others. After he had lit his fuse and climbed out of the trench, he banged his leg on a rock that was sticking out of the dirt. He had an adrenaline dump at the time, and hardly noticed. Only after several minutes did he notice the pain. With his arm in a make shift sling, he walked on with determination. They marched as fast as the slowest person, each occasionally glancing behind them for any pursuit. They soon passed an old farm house, but did not dare stop. Right after passing the house they saw the road that led up to the top of a plateau. After that, there was flat land, and then after that, more rolling hills and the protection of trees and their home.

Going up the hill was not too bad, considering that they went up in elevation about a hundred feet. Once they got to the top they headed off the road to the nearest trees.

They gratefully took a short break while they ate and drank the last of their supplies. The shelter was only a mile away from where they sat. As they were resting, they heard the sound of an engine.

Lucky was the first to hear the truck, and perked his ears up. Connie was sitting beside him and noticed his head snapping up. She was the next one to hear it. She quickly said, "everybody get down. A vehicle is coming."

Connie held onto Lucky as they all flattened behind the trees. Several seconds later a truck came up the same road they had been on. It stopped several yards passed where they left the road. They could see the Boss behind the wheel. The other men got out and studied the dirt road. They watched them as they walked back until they saw where their tracks left the road.

Dane whispered loudly, "Everybody move now! Stay low and try not to leave any tracks. Connie make sure you keep the dog with you. Wayne and Chris cover our retreat. If they follow our prints, shoot to kill."

Everyone complied quickly. As soon as they put more of the evergreens between them and their followers, they rose up and headed out quickly. They stepped on the field grass when they could, trying to avoid leaving tracks in the dirt. Wayne and Chris lay down under the nearest tree and readied their weapons.

The men on the side of the road could easily see the foot prints, as well as a single set of tire prints in the hard, but dusty, road. The scrub grass was not very tall and did not cover all of the ground, so tracking would not be too hard. Two of them knelt down and studied the direction the tracks were going. They stood up and one of them made the mistake of pointing at the trees where the tracks went. He suddenly dropped to the ground. A split second later came the unmistakable sound of a rifle. Then another of the men fell at their feet. The rest quickly scrambled for cover behind the truck. They fumbled with their weapons and started firing randomly into the trees.

After the first two fell, Wayne and Chris crawled backwards, then quickly got up and ran for it. They quickly dodged around some trees as they caught up with the others. A small tree branch dropped right behind Chris as he ran around a tree.

The Boss slouched down inside the cab as well as he could.

"Shoot them! Shoot them, damn it!" He screamed.

The men beside the truck poured bullet after bullet into the area where the sound of the rifles came. There were no more shots coming from the area, so their enemies were either dead or escaped. Unfortunately for them, the two that died were the only military men in the group and the Boss knew it. The reality of what they were doing started to sink in.

Tony, the eighteen year old, started shaking uncontrollably.

"Let's go back now," he said with his voice shaking.

"*No*!" The Boss said firmly. "We will *not* let them get away! They just killed two of our Chosen Ones, and they will *pay*!" That seemed to get the spark of anger going to just enough to overcome his fear.

After quickly picking up the two dropped weapons, the Boss got in the front of the truck and sat low on the seat, just so he could see out of the front window. The others got in the back and laid down. He drove slowly drove up to the trees and stopped. He was really relieved when no gun shots rang out.

They all got out and surveyed the area where their foes had been hiding. They found where their ambushers hid while they murdered two of their men. After looking around a little bit they could see where two people had crawled away from the tree. There were marks in the dirt where they had gotten up and ran off through the trees. After that the tracks got really hard to follow. The Boss decided that it would be suicide to follow them and they drove back to the road and continued to follow the tire tracks.

After running a short distance, Wayne and Chris caught up to the others. They all continued to parallel the road while being hidden by the trees. As they stopped to catch their breath, they could hear the truck continuing up the road.

"They're following the truck tracks," said Connie as she realized where the truck was headed. After several months of driving up to the shelter from the road, it was inevitable that they would wear down the grass. They tried to take a slightly different route up to the shelter, but they could only go so many different ways through the trees to get there. For diligent hunters, it would be easy to find.

The trees got closer together as they made their way away from the flattened farmland. The evergreen trees were fat and squat and provided lots of cover. The closer they got to their home, the more deciduous trees they started to see.

They were passing in front of the Marshall's house when Dane stopped. His leg and arm were hurting, and he was at the last of his endurance.

"I'm going to have to wait here," he said with a pale face. "I have to rest for a while."

"Me too," said Frank. His fingers were bloody where he pressed his hand against the right side of his ribs.

Connie was suddenly at his side. He carefully sat down on the front steps of the house. She knew her father well. He would not complain about the pain unless it was really bad. She pulled his hand away to check the wound. Blood slowly seeped from a three-inch gash that looked like it just missed his ribs.

"We need to get him inside," she said as she stood up. "We need to stop that bleeding."

Dane refused help into the house, so Wayne and Connie helped Frank. The others kept watch as they went into the house.

Wayne quickly undid the hidden door and almost had to carry Frank down the stairs. He was weak from blood loss, but still did not complain.

"Why didn't you say anything, Frank?" Wayne said with a little anger. "You could have bled to death."

"I couldn't slow you down," he gasped as his daughter pulled his shirt away from the clotting blood. "If anyone got hurt again because of me, well...I...just couldn't bear it."

The rest of the group came downstairs to see how it was going.

Wayne knew that the people following their truck tracks would find their shelter. "I need someone to go with me to the shelter. If they've gotten inside, they will most likely try to destroy it. I can't let that happen," he said with a dark face.

The shelter that became their home was Wayne's life achievement. He had many dreams of things he wanted to do, but the shelter was the one thing he managed to complete. It not only sheltered them from the aftermath of the fall of man, but also brought him inner peace and helped bring out his spirituality. Every time he went out after the storms he appreciated nature and her animals even more. He felt his being expand beyond the shriveled up thing that it was while humanity destroyed their surroundings and each other.

"Chris, are you up to coming with me?" He got a nod from

him, so he turned to Susan. "What about you?" She stood up with her weapon ready. "Count me in," she said bravely.

"I'm coming too," Connie said as she stood up. "Perra can take care of these two."

Perra nodded her agreement as she opened up a first-aid kit and started to clean the wound.

June was beside Frank's side as she looked up. "I'm sorry, but I don't know anything about shooting a gun, much less shooting at a person. I'll stay here and help look after these two.

"OK," said Wayne. "Once these guys are taken care of, try to dig behind that wall at the bottom of the stairs. I have a feeling that there is a gun cabinet in there somewhere."

"Where are we supposed to put all of that stuff?" Perra asked.

"Try stacking it in the bathroom, then maybe one of the isles. We might have to be able to use that small window in the wall in case they get inside this shelter. We have no other place to go that is safe.

As the two women were taking care of the two men, Wayne changed out the batteries in the radios. As he squeezed his way around the four people in the isle, his brother said softly, "Be careful Wayne."

Wayne stopped and made eye contact with his older brother. He smiled briefly and nodded, then turned and followed the others up the stairs.

Lucky started to head up the steps as his people were leaving. "Sorry Lucky, but you need to stay," Wayne said. The dog understood the word "stay", so he stayed on the steps looking up at Wayne with his sad eyes. "Maybe next time," he said as he closed the door behind him.

As soon as Perra got Frank cleaned up and bandaged, she gave him some pain pills. Dane said he did not need anything.

June and Perra started in on the stacks of food, clothing and other gear that filled the space Wayne said he needed cleared. They moved a few dozen items before Dane got up and started helping.

"You need to rest," Perra said as she looked up at him.

"I know," he said, "but I can't just let you two do all the work when I still have one good arm. I can at least carry something small."

Perra stood her ground in front of him. She pondered for second, then, "Let me give you something for the pain first."

Dane grumbled as she nosed through the first-aid kit. She brought him two pills and some water, which he took immediately.

Frank painfully shuffled out of the way and sat on some boxes by the kitchenette.

Dane started loading up the women, so they could make trips to the bathroom. They did not have much room, so they put as much as they could under the sink, on top of the toilet, and then in the shower stall. They were careful to stack it so it would not fall.

They made steady progress once Dane started making a narrow path behind the narrow wall. After about twenty-five minutes, he complained of dizziness and went to sit down on the floor beside Frank. Within several minutes, he was asleep.

Perra had a smug look as she continued working.

June looked somewhat confused at her attitude. "What did you give him?"

She grunted as she lifted two heavy boxes of preserved food, "Sleeping pills. He was in no shape to help us. I was afraid that he could have made his injuries worse."

June smiled a mischievous smile as if she were an accomplice. She was truly starting to like this quiet little lady.

They quickly cleared an area of twenty square feet behind the small wall facing the stairs. They found the missing stash of weapons in a regular metal cabinet. It was located on the back wall, in the corner and facing the stairs. It had a few high powered hunting rifles with scopes, as well as a few smaller caliber hunting rifles. What surprised them was the amount of bullets that were stacked up. The whole thing was almost full.

Frank made his way over to see what they found. He stood there with a grimace on his face. "Don't even *ask* if I want anything for pain," he said with a glare at Perra.

Both of the women just looked at each other and shared a knowing smile.

Wayne put the boards back on the wall as the others waited in the kitchen. He wanted to plan their next move before they headed out. He knew that Connie knew their hand signals and needed to let the other two know. He also had to insist on absolute silence as they tracked their trackers. One radio would go to Wayne and Chris, and the other one to the other two. After seeing Chris almost lose it the day before, he needed to make sure he kept him with him. So far he seemed to be doing well, despite the fact that just a half hour ago he had to kill a man for the first time in his life.

They soon left the house through the back door. Connie and Susan would bring up the rear. They would only use the radios if they got separated. Wayne was going to lead them fairly close to the road. If the others could follow their tire tracks, they could follow theirs. He did not like exposing himself, but he had to know where they went.

Connie and Susan were to stay back just far enough to keep the two men in sight.

It was nearing noon as they made their way through the stubby trees. The grass was dry now that the sun had come up, but they still managed to be extremely quiet.

Wayne knelt down beside a tree that the narrow road went by. He could clearly see two sets of tire tracks in the dirt. He backtracked several yards and continued following the road at that distance. Every hundred yards he slowly went back to the road to make sure the others had not left it.

As they drew closer to the shelter, Wayne slowed his pace and eventually stopped for a few seconds, listening hard. His worst fears were confirmed. His pulse started to pound when he saw the truck pulled up to the fake bunker. Two of the men were standing on the other side of the truck with their weapons pointed down the way they came. Little did they know that Wayne was watching them from ninety degrees from where they were focusing their attention.

It did not take long for the Boss to come out of the shelter with a box of food and supplies. He was in a hurry and quickly put the box in the back and made another trip inside.

Wayne was furious. In their haste to get Connie back, they must have left the inside door unsecured. He could not remember who came out last, but right now that was the least of his worries. The two men on watch occasionally shifted their attention in his direction, if only briefly.

As Wayne and Chris were watching the others raid their supplies, Connie and Susan were watching their boots as they stuck out from under a pine tree. Connie found a warm, sunny place to kneel down, and gladly did so. Susan, who was several yards away, wanted to see what the guys were looking at. They had not given any signals yet, so she slowly inched her way around the south side of a tree. She figured she would only be out of sight of Connie for a few seconds at most, and it would not hurt anything.

As she saw Connie kneel down and look intently in the direction of their two men, she saw what she thought a gnarled branch that lay on the ground. Minding it no heed, she went to brush it out of the way with her toe. A split second later the sunbathing rattlesnake quickly sank its fangs into her calf.

To the men raiding their enemies' home, this was the best revenge they could get away with, besides killing the murderers that had tried to destroy their home. Finding the hidden shelter was not just an enormous surprise, but almost laughably easy. The tire tracks took them right to the shelter. Originally they were stumped at the small shelter sticking out of the hillside, but upon a closer look, the back wall had a straight-vertical crack all along the back-left corner. A vigorous push and they were stunned with what they found. They brought an extra can of gas and were about to dump it on the beds, light it, and then leave when the Boss decided to load up before anyone arrived. He posted two men outside, then headed for the food. It had been a long time since he had canned fruit.

With the truck backed up to the shelter, the two men outside had an easy line of sight back the way they came. They figured that anyone arriving would come in the same basic direction, and stood guard as such. After a few minutes of waiting outside, the tension seemed to gather. They knew their foes would be arriving at any time now and, in fact, thought them late. As they stood there anticipating an attack, the calm and quiet afternoon was suddenly interrupted with a blood- curdling scream.

Chris' pulse was up as he tried to steady his nerves. He had been too busy to think much after killing a man for the first time in his life. After they had stopped off at the house, he had time to think about it. A wash of emotion threatened to overwhelm him as they made their way to another possible conflict. After slowly crawling his way under the tree and took aim at the intruders, his hands started to shake so badly that he could hardly see anything in the scope. After a few minutes of trying to slow his breathing, he finally managed to hold the rifle almost steady.

When the scream came, Chris recognized it immediately. He had a bead on one of the guys and was waiting for the signal from Wayne when the unexpected scream came, causing him to jump and almost squeeze off a round. With his love in danger, he hardly felt the scratch of low branches as he quickly backed up and headed toward the sound.

Wayne froze when he heard the sound. He did not want to kill unnecessarily, especially when he had such an impressionable young man like Chris watching. The men would have been easy to drop, but the other two were still inside with the rest of their weapons, ammunition and supplies. The place was built to be easily defended from intruders. It was a fact that he was proud of, but at the moment found it ironic.

When Chris scrambled out from under the tree, the two men immediately reacted by pointing in their direction and started firing. Wayne took out the one with the large caliber hunting rifle before the other ducked, but he could see below the truck where he was hiding. One leg was showing from behind the tire, so he put a round in the meatiest part. The man immediately dropped to the ground in agony. He could see the Boss and another man come to the door way with their weapons up. They took a few wild shots and headed for the driver's door. They clumsily pulled the injured man in as they jumped inside. The man on the ground had a hole in the middle of his forehead and was obviously dead.

Connie nearly peed her pants as she heard Susan. The younger woman was out of sight, but quickly came into view while limping towards her. Her face was as white as a ghost.

Connie moved towards her in a crouch as the bullets started flying. She nearly tackled the teenager as they got close enough, trying to get her as low as possible. Susan was holding her calf and was clearly terrified, not to mention in pain.

With trees all around and no idea what was going on, Connie said, "Calm down Susan, and for Christ's sake keep quiet."

"I got bit by a rattlesnake," she said while almost hyperventilating.

Connie knew that she was not in a position to berate the teenager for wondering off, especially with armed men around. She quickly unhooked her belt and wrapped it a few inches above the bite marks. After she had it wrapped around a few times, she slid the end under and looped it around the first part a few more times. She then looked around for anything to hide behind. They made it several more yards when Chris came running around a tree. His face had a mix of emotions as his eyes quickly took in the small stain on Susan's pant leg. He quickly helped her, so they could put some distance between them and the intruders.

Chris felt extremely guilty at leaving Wayne, but his instinct to protect Susan over rode his need to stay with Wayne.

"Let's get her back to the house," he said as they tried to jog.

"What about Wayne?" Connie said, looking back towards the shelter.

Chris was about to answer when a meaty thud came from his direction. A split second later a few shots rang out. He gave a small jerk, wavered a little, and with a confused look on his face dropped to the ground, taking Susan with him as he fell.

When Wayne came into view, he was stooped over and back tracking as best he could. When he glanced behind him and saw the two teens tangled up on the ground, he quickly came over.

Connie was at Chris' side and nearly in tears. She quickly rolled him on his back to assess the damage. His shirt had a neat hole in it near the seam by his right shoulder. She quickly tore the hole bigger, so she could see the wound better.

"Help me roll him on his side," she said to Susan.

Susan was near hysterical as she saw the blood seeping into his shirt, but she complied.

All three of them rolled Chris onto his left side as his mother checked for an exit wound. She sighed a huge sigh of relief when she saw a similar hole in his back. It appeared to have missed the bones.

Wayne crouched down and was nervously watching for any signs of pursuit as Connie tried to stop the flow of blood.

Susan was crying and being a huge distraction. Wayne quietly said through clenched jaws, "Quiet down damn it!"

She jerked as if slapped, and stopped sobbing.

Wayne heard the truck rapidly heading toward the dirt road. He cupped his hands behind his ears, so he could follow it as it headed back the way they came.

Wayne quickly studied the two women and said, "Let's get him back to the others."

"Why not take him to our shelter?" Connie asked. "It's just through those trees."

"Because there's strength in numbers, and also because they shot my radio," he said holding it up to show the bullet hole in it. "We have no way to let them know what is going on."

Connie reached for her radio. "We can use...oh no." She patted the place where the radio used to be, but it was gone. It had been clipped to her belt.

"We don't have the time anyway," Connie said desperately. "A piece of his shirt went in with the bullet. We need to get that out as soon as possible, and while he is still unconscious. If he wakes up too soon, we'll play hell trying to get it out."

"All right, but we need to move now. Susan, get his rifle and keep a lookout for that truck." She accepted their rifles, as well.

With Wayne and Susan on either side, they managed to get under each shoulder, so they could drag him easier. Even though they only had a hundred yards to go, they were both winded by the time they reached the open doorway.

Susan nearly fainted as she saw the hole in the forehead of the man by the entryway.

They dragged Chris in and soon had him on the nearest bed. Wayne said, "Susan, get the big first-aid kit by the armory, then secure the door."

When Wayne had planned the shelter and the hundreds of things they would need for it, he made sure he had items that would be needed for just this occasion. The scalpels and sewing supplies were still in their sterile containers, so the only thing they needed to sterilize was Chris' skin.

When Chris was crawling under the trees, he got his clothes extremely dirty. When the bullet went through, it carried the contamination with it, minute as it was.

Wayne quickly opened the case and pulled out a bottle of rubbing alcohol. He poured it over Connie's hands, then his hands, and grabbed a sealed bag of operating gloves. She held her hands up as Wayne carefully pulled the gloves out, then helped her put them on.

Susan sat on the other side of the double sized bed and checked out her bite. Meanwhile, the others worked on her fiancé. She did not want to see what they were doing. She nearly cried out when she saw the red, puffy puncture wounds on her leg.

After Wayne had handed her the scalpel, Connie made a small incision across the wound. She did not go very deep on the first pass. She wanted to widen the entry to the wound, so she could go deeper with the long, thin tweezers. After several times of dipping in and retrieving nothing, she deepened the cut and tried again. After a few more tries, she pulled out a small, round piece of cloth. She quickly poured more alcohol on the wound and wiped up the mess. Wayne had another sealed bag with a sewing needle and thread. He opened it without touching the contents, and then laid it down for Connie to use. After sewing up the front of his shoulder, they rolled him onto his left side.

Wayne used sharp scissors to cut the shirt away from the area. He tossed the piece of shirt on the floor, then poured more alcohol on the small hole. He carefully cleaned the wound, then moved and let Connie sew it up. He cleaned his hands and dug into the medical kit again.

He found the little yellow container and took it to the other side of the bed, where Susan was sitting. He opened the plastic top and took out the contents.

"This may hurt, so try not to move. We may be too late to get most of the poison out, but this should help." He gently wiped the area with a clean gauze pad soaked with water. Then he pulled out a small suction cup and put it over one of the small holes. There were two suction cups in the kit, so he used the next one for the other hole.

Susan winced but said nothing. Lucky for her it did not appear that much venom was injected when the snake bit her.

Wayne stood up and looked at the two injured people. There was nothing more he could do, and stood there shaking his head. He looked around at the mess inside their home. A box with several jars of canned food had been dropped on the floor. Another box with spices and a few boxes of ammunition lay on its side by the door. Even though he wanted to clean up the mess, Wayne still needed to get back to the others, just in case they were discovered.

"There's nothing more for me to do here. I'm going to head back to the others. Make sure you re-secure the inner door when I leave. When I come back, I will come through one of the upper hatches."

Connie came over and with tears in her eyes, gave him a hug. "Thanks for helping me with Chris." She turned and looked down at her son. "I don't know what I would do if I lost him again." Her shoulders shook as she quietly cried. Wayne patted her on the shoulder, then walked over to his weapon. He shouldered it and turned back to the charcoal-smeared faces that were facing him.

"I shouldn't be gone more than a few hours. Whatever you do, do not follow me."

The two scared women simply looked at him with wide eyes and nodded.

"Make sure you secure this door after I leave," he said again.

As Wayne stepped through the inner door, he waited for it to close. When he heard the satisfying "thunk" of the rebar-reinforced block of concrete go into its place, he headed to the outer door. He patiently scanned the area for any movement, listening for any signs of the three men.

He wanted Connie to come with him, but she was needed here more than he needed her. After many years of let downs, he knew he was better off going alone. People let you down and, for the most part, could not be trusted. It was the main reason why he survived when most of the population of Earth had died. His planning of the shelter was a direct result of his distrust of society, of his isolation for so many years. Nature was pure and peaceful, albeit dangerous for the untrained. Most men seemed out of place and unable to blend in with their surrounds, with their brothers of skin, fur and feather. Now his shelter, his home, had been defiled too.

After several minutes of hearing and seeing nothing unusual, he headed for the body lying in the grass. He learned long ago not to look at personal items in wallets and pockets, or to try and identify with the body as a person with a family, feelings, and history. The feelings of guilt and remorse tore him up the first few times he had to kill another human being. After talking with Dane, he began to stop thinking of the body as a person, but as nothing more than a dead animal. It was better to think that way than carry around the burden of remorse.

Stooping down, Wayne quickly grabbed the high-powered rifle and shouldered it. He checked a few pockets for more rounds and came up with a battered box with a few shells in it. He retreated to the shelter and pulled the magazine out, then loaded the remaining rounds into it. After making sure the safety was on, he stepped out and closed the door.

He noticed the faint trails leading up to the shelter. They tried to avoid leaving a permanent road, but as many times as they left and returned throughout the summer, they eventually left several trails to their home.

He had originally planned to skirt the large rocks and fallen debris along the bottom of the plateau, but after thinking about it for a few seconds, decided to try and find out where the three men went. He stealthily walked from tree to tree, paused, then moved further down the grassy slope.

Wayne sighed as he realized that even though you try your best to plan for the future, there were just too many ways to get tripped up. Murphy's Law *always* found a way.

Although he did not have Danes' military training, he had a heightened sense of reality as he zigzagged from tree to tree. The short, squat Pinon trees were spread just far enough that he had to risk exposing himself to get to the next one.

The late fall afternoon had the calm and quiet of a restful spring day. It seemed so surreal to Wayne as he made his way to the next tree. The shade was cool, but the sun was warm on the left side of his face and neck as he headed west. He made sure to keep an eye out for any basking snakes.

He could clearly see both tracks of the truck, plus the

older and deeper tracks from their truck. He continued on carefully.

His greatest fear was that they had stopped, and were back-tracking on foot. With one man wounded, that would still leave two fully armed men. *But*, he thought, *they would have to be crazy to keep coming after them*. Especially since half of them were dead and one man badly hurt. At this point, Wayne would not even try to figure out their mind set. He just planned as if they were still hunting for him and his companions.

Chapter 28
One Crazy Man

The three men in the truck were scared out of their wits and not thinking straight. After their buddy had his brains blown out, they headed down the road at break-neck speed. After a half mile and almost crashing into a tree, some reasoning came back into the driver, Tony.

The man with the wound screamed and yelled. The Boss, next to the passenger door, finally snapped and punched him in the jaw, knocking him out. In his state of mind, he did not bother to try and help him, or even notice the hole in his buddies calf, or the pool of blood on the floor-board. In his crazed state, all he could think of was about killing the invaders, of taking their women and raping them, and then slowly butchering them. He would make them *pay* for killing his flock, his Chosen Ones.

"Tony, stop," he exclaimed. "We can't leave until we get them for what they've done."

"There's too many of them," Tony replied. "They've killed half of us, and Jim has a hole in his leg. They will kill us all," he said with spittle flying.

The Boss calmly sat back in his seat and said quietly, "Stop now."

"I can't," he said desperately. They will kill us."

"Stop, or *I* will kill you," he said, pointing his rifle at him.

Tony stopped only after turning and seeing the rifle barrel pointed at his forehead. He had just passed a driveway heading up the slight incline. He kept repeating, "they're going to kill us. They're gonna kill us all!"

"Grab your weapon and follow me, we can find them. Then we'll sneak up on them. We *will* find them!"

Tony got out but kept up his rant. He started shaking his head and backed away from the truck.

"Where are you going?"

The only reply was, "They're going to kill us all!"

"Coward!" Shouted the Boss. A second later he squeezed the trigger and put a bullet through Tony's chest. *A coward cannot be one of the Chosen,* he rationalized.

The sound inside the cab of the small truck was deafening, and he could not hear much for a few minutes. He did not hear the waxy faced man that slumped over on the seat exhale his last breath. Nor did he notice the large pool of blood that had soaked his hiking shoes. He grabbed the other two weapons, got out of the truck and walked into the sparsely wooded area.

As Wayne was getting close to the Marshall's house, he could almost feel the tension emanating from the surrounding area. The birds had gone quiet just before he heard a muffled gun shot. He was so tense that he flattened himself on the ground behind a tree before realizing that the sound came from the direction of the main road, and not the house. He stayed where he was for several minutes, but saw nothing. He slowly got up and checked out the house. It appeared the same as before, *so hopefully,* he thought, *those crazy bastard's had not found the place yet.* He stood up and made his way to the house. He went up the steps and stopped by the door. He peeked inside, then turned around to see if anyone was approaching. He saw something that looked like the top of a man's head behind a tree, so he quickly opened the door and stepped inside.

After walking north for a few minutes, the Boss came across an old dirt driveway. He decided to follow it up and, as he came into sight of a house, he saw a man with an unusually dirty face. He was wearing camouflage clothes and had two weapons. An evil grin spread across his face. He lifted his weapon and dropped to one knee. In doing so he lost sight of his enemy, so he shuffled to the side and peered through the tree branches. He quickly shifted his rifle to get a shot, but the other man disappeared into the house. Aiming at where he though the man would be, he thumbed off the safety and fired his weapon.

Wayne stepped in and quickly ducked down, then moved to the large living room window five feet to his left. He slowly peeked out at where he thought he saw someone a few seconds ago. He slowly peeked around the window sill. Suddenly a piece of the wall blew out where he had just been. He wanted to return fire, but he could not see where the man was. He decided to crawl across the room and into the kitchen when several more bullets blew holes in the living room wall. Drywall and small pieces of insulation littered the hardwood floor as he low crawled his way into the next room. The two rifles came off his shoulders, so he dragged them by their straps. Getting safely to the kitchen, he stood up and went into the pantry. A few seconds later he heard shots coming from the kitchen. When he had closed the door behind him, the L..E.D. lights went out. He felt around until he found the small timer on the wall. When he twisted it, the lights came back on. As they did, Wayne felt an enormous blow to his leg, which knocked him against the wall. The bullet had gone through the meaty part of his right thigh. Clenching his teeth, he managed to get the inside door open. He nearly passed out as he slowly went down the stairs.

"We've got company," he called out, "and he's not very nice."

The Boss' foe was either dead or playing possum. *That's OK*, he thought, *I'll shoot you again just to make sure you are dead!*. He ran up to the doorway of the house and peeked in the small window. He could see scuff marks in the dust, and saw Wayne's feet disappear around a door way. The coward had crawled away! His contemptuous grin spread even further.

"I'm going to kill you!" He backed away from the door, then kicked it in. Wood splinters added to the mess on the floor. He quickly entered the room with his rifle aimed where he saw Wayne go into. He ran over to the doorway where the scuff marks disappeared. The room was empty.

"Interesting," he said. He suddenly saw the pantry door. "I have you now! Are you ready to die?" He fired a round into the door and tried to fire another, but the weapon was empty. He dropped that weapon and took the other one off his shoulder. After firing two more shots into the door and wall, he whipped it open. He jumped in with his rifle ready, but the room was empty except for a few wide boards leaning against a wall.

"Hmm... where did you go?" He asked with a sly look.

After his eyes adjusted to the low-light level, he looked down at the floor. He could make out a few drops of blood. Then he noticed that the dust had many fresh foot prints in the small room, but why? He walked forward several feet and knelt down by the wall. He could make out some footprints that led into the wall. He stood up and banged his head on one of the shelving brackets, causing him to lose balance. He grabbed for the nearest bracket... and the wall moved outward.

"You people are full of surprises. Are you ready to die now?" He yelled. He opened the door enough to see what was behind it. He saw his foe at the bottom of the stairs and quickly fired. The chips from the concrete pelted Wayne's right arm and shoulder. The Boss grinned again as he yelled down the stairs, "Now it's time to die, coward. You have nowhere else to run." He cautiously continued down the stairs, aiming his weapon.

After he got to the fourth step a voice rang out, "Stop and leave or die."

Wayne was standing with the barrel of his rifle resting in the small square hole of the wall. He bent down painfully to aim correctly, but had a clear view of the intruder. He could clearly see it was the Boss. His hair was a mess, but it did not compare to the look on his face, or the crazed look in his eyes. The man was actually smiling!

"The only one to die is you, coward!" His eyes were still getting used to the low light, but he could clearly see a small opening in the wall at the bottom of the stairs. Something was sticking out of it. His eyes widened as he understood what was sticking out at him. He quickly aimed his weapon and fired.

At almost the same instant, Wayne put a bullet through his heart. A few pieces of concrete ricocheted through the hole and cut his cheek but was otherwise okay. The intruder dropped like a rag doll and tumbled down the stairs. A few more shots from a different direction tore into him as he lay there in a crumpled heap.

Wayne wiped the blood from his face. He slowly limped around the barrier. He knew the Boss could not have survived the shots, but was cautious regardless.

He lay crumpled up against the wall with his neck at an odd angle. The half-opened eyes were sightless as Wayne checked for a pulse. He could not find one, so he carefully made his way up the steps.

Frank quickly joined him as they made their way out of the pantry, and then into the kitchen. They searched the house, but did not find anyone else, so they went back down into the shelter.

As they came back down the stairs, Perra and June came out of hiding. Perra was holding her .22 long rifle and looking terrified. Streaks of fresh tears showed on her puffy cheeks. June looked disheveled and tired but was okay.

Perra saw the blood on Wayne's pant leg and let out a terrified moan.

"You're hurt," she cried.

Wayne started to get light headed, and suddenly everyone was at his side. Many strong hands helped him sit down. Perra was too terrified to think of stopping the flow of blood. June grabbed the first-aid kit, opened it and got something to press against the slow flow of blood. Perra shook herself out her stupor and helped. She pressed a pad against the hole on the other side of his leg.

Lucky was busy sniffing the body.

Dane had awakened with the sound of the gun fire and

was up, but still groggy. He still was not up to helping and was extremely grumpy, especially when he realized that the pills Perra gave him were not for pain. He would have to keep a closer eye on that little trickster. He saw Wayne laying in an isle with a bloody leg, which woke him up immediately. His younger brother was pale but awake. He felt better knowing that Wayne was in capable hands.

After cutting the pant leg off Wayne, they were better able to get him cleaned up. By then, the shock wore off and the pain too much. Wayne finally passed out. The pads on both sides of his leg soon became soaked, so they added a folded wash cloth to each side. Once they wrapped up his leg, the two women turned to the minor wounds on his face, right arm, and shoulder.

It took four of them to man-handle the body up the stairs. They wanted to get it out before it bled all over the place. The stairs were not very wide, but after much jostling, huffing and puffing, they got it out of the shelter. They took the thin body of the Boss out through the back door and dumped it several yards into the trees. They could bury him later, once they knew that the area was safe. Dane had to keep shooing the dog away from the body.

They all went back down stairs where they found Wayne awake. Perra immediately gave him a cup of water and pain pills. He updated them on the events earlier.

Perra and June cleaned up the bloody mess from the Boss. They used a few towels and had to make repeated trips to the bathroom sink to squeeze them out.

"We need to regroup." Frank said. "We'll be stronger together Besides that, I'm really worried about Chris. If that wound gets infected, he'll be in trouble. That goes for you too. Do you have any antibiotics?" He asked Wayne.

"No, I don't have anything for infections inside the body. I only got antibiotics for topical applications."

"Then let's hope that's all we will need," Frank said tiredly.

"We should check to make sure the others are gone, Wayne said, changing the subject. By my count, there should be two more men out there somewhere, and one is hurt."

They decided it would be best to grab something to eat, since it had been a few hours since breakfast. Wayne was especially hungry since he had expended so much energy going to, and returning from, their shelter.

They rummaged through the canned food and came up with peaches and vegetable stew with meat. Perra managed to find some bowls and silverware in the kitchenette. They did not bother to heat the stew, since they felt that time was against them.

Soon after they finished eating and using the bathroom Dane and Frank grabbed their weapons, the two remaining radios, and headed out. They put the boards back on the brackets and, rechecking the house, went out the back door.

Frank grimaced once in a while, but did not complain as they went from tree to tree, checking to make sure the area was clear. Dane was just as stoic. They made long sweeping zigzags as they made their way to the road.

Once they located the truck, they spent the next several minutes making sure the area was clear. They slowly circled around the truck and found one of the men lying on his back. It was clear that he was dead. They slowly approached the truck, and they found the other one slumped over on his side. He too was dead. Even though six men had lost their lives, they felt relieved now that the threat was gone.

After shutting off the engine, they pulled the body out of the truck and laid him next to the other man, who could not have been out of his teens. They then turned their attention to the truck. The pool of blood was congealing and smelled metallic. They threw in lots of soft, powdery dirt to soak it up, then looked for something to use for a shovel. After searching the area for something to use, they ended up using their hands to scoop out the bloody mess. Once they got most of it out, they threw in more dirt to help soak up the rest of the blood, but this time they left it there. There would be time enough later to clean the carpet, or just tear it out.

Dane drove back to the house in silence. Their ordeal was over for now, but the killing of men was a heavy burden to bear, even in a survival situation. He did not look forward to their last task. It was no matter that they tried to kill him and his family, they now had to bury the bodies. For now, it could wait.

After telling the others of their findings, they decided to get back to the shelter with the others. They made a makeshift crutch for Wayne. Lucky gladly jumped in the back of the truck, just before they headed down the dusty road.

Dane pulled up to their home and went up to the left escape hatch. He almost forgot to look around for prying eyes before opening up the hatch. All of the gun fire earlier could have brought unwanted visitors.

As he waited for Dane to open the shelter door, a suddenly thought hit Wayne. As he sat there staring into the familiar trees and distant mountains, it occurred how much things had changed, and at the same time, how things were still the same. Their predictable lives while hiding away in the shelter seemed so long ago but was only several months before. They had been so cautious for so long, and when they let their guard down, it had cost them dearly.

He had hoped that people would change for the better when things got bad, but men were men and probably would not change for many more thousands of years, if then. The immensity of their life changes almost overwhelmed him then, as he sat beside the fake boulder. So much carnage, so much death and destruction, and all mainly because of greed. Because of an inability to let others live their own lives. Man had to control everything, from plants and seeds, energy, nature, the Earth itself, and especially other men. Wayne had long ago wished that man could live and let live, but it did not seem to be in their nature. How and why we came to be such violent creatures, was beyond him. *How can we create such beauty, but be so ugly at the same time*? He wondered for the thousandth time.

Dane, just as careful about his surroundings as his brother, looked around for a few seconds, then reached down and unlatched the lid. He climbed down and re-latched it, while calling out to those inside the shelter that all was clear. The lower hatch opened, so he climbed down to greet Connie. She had a look of relief, also looked worried.

"How are Chris and Susan?" He asked, turning to face her.

"Chris woke up in a lot of pain and is starting to run a fever. So I loaded him up on pain pills and a few sleeping pills, so at least we don't have to hear him moan. Susan's leg isn't much better, but I don't think the snake injected much poison."

"I have the others waiting to come in," he said, then started down the stairs. He asked Susan how she was doing as he went by to unlock the inner door. She was still sitting in the same place as when Wayne left a few hours before. He barely heard her reply. He realized that she might be in shock.

As they unloaded and headed into the shelter, Perra and June saw the body lying several feet from the entrance. Perra gulped and quickly made her way inside. June saw the disfigured head and threw up. Frank quickly blocked her view and helped her inside. He had to call the dog away from the body as they went inside and closed the door.

CHAPTER 29
ANOTHER TRIP

They were all exhausted from their ordeal and mainly wanted to clean up and get some sleep. The hot water was ready, so Wayne took a spit bath while Perra showered, then the other women took quick showers. When it was Franks turn, he did not care that the hot water was gone and took a cool shower. They had to wait another hour before there was enough hot water, and after the next few showers, the sun was too low to heat any more water.

Only a few of them stayed up long enough to eat something before finding some place to sleep. There were only three beds and eight people. Susan slept beside Chris while Wayne, Perra and June slept on another. Dane and Connie slept on one bed while Frank grabbed some blankets and headed upstairs to sleep on the floor. At least he had Lucky by his side.

They woke up late, and most of them were very sore. Their moods picked up as they smelled a delightful odor. Perra and June had awoken early and made pancakes. It was not fancy, but after the previous two days' exertions and cold food, it made all of their mouths water. Everyone except for Chris.

Chris woke up in a cold sweat. His clothes lay plastered to his skin, and he was in a great deal of pain. The area surrounding the entry wound was a nasty red and had a foul odor to it. He could hardly move without screaming out in pain. The mood quickly died down with everyone being very concerned for him.

Wayne too was starting to get a fever.

"We have to do something," Connie nearly wept. Do you have anything to fight an infection?"

"I have some old amoxicillin," Wayne said slowly, "but I don't know if it's still good. Check to see when the expiration date ended." Connie went to find it and returned discouraged. It had expired two years previous.

"It's better than nothing." Susan said as she sat by Chris holding his hand.

"Lets hope so. If it doesn't do anything in the next few days, we'll need to find a hospital and see if they have any injectable antibiotics. I'm just not sure how long the shelf life is, but hopefully it's longer than these pills," Connie said looking at the label.

Perra made some meat broth for Chris to drink. She let it cool for a while before she gave it to him. She did not want to add insult to injury by burning his tongue. He was feverish, but gladly accepted the warm fluid. After he had finished, he asked for cold water.

They decided that he needed the saline solution drip when he kept asking for water. He seemed to be sweating it out faster than he was drinking it. Wayne fared better.

Early the next day they could not tell if the antibiotics

were working or not. They were going to keep up the dosage, three times per day and were going to wait another day, maybe two at the most.

Dane, Connie, and Perra went out to take care of the bodies.

"I'm sorry," June said, "but I have such a weak stomach that if I try to help you I will be sick for a week." She looked as if she were going to puke just talking about it.

"That's okay," Perra sympathized. "We can take care of it, but you will owe us a big meal for when we get back," she said with a slight twinkle in her eyes.

The three of them quietly grabbed a few shovels, some food and water and slipped out with the sun freshly up.

They pulled the body of the man by their home several yards away, and behind a rotund evergreen. Dane and Connie started digging as Perra struggled with anything useful that was still on the body. They learned a while back that many of the abandoned houses had plenty of clothing they could use. Most of the clothing would fit at least one of them. It was the shoes that they needed most, if they fit, and most likely would be the only thing they took from the dead men. Belts and hats were a second priority, since they seemed to be in short supply.

They often talked of trying to make a run into one of the larger cities to see if any clothing were left. Wayne had planned well enough, but underwear, bras and socks wore out much faster than outer clothing. They figured that if they needed to go, those were the items they would try and find first. They were not desperate enough to take used under clothes.

It took over a half hour to get deep enough to keep animals from digging the body up. With hardly a word, they pulled the corpse up beside the hole and rolled it inside. The fleshy plop almost got to Perra, but she was getting used to the thought of dead people by now. She helped push the dirt back on top and packed it down. She insisted on putting something at the head of the grave, even if just to mark it. After she had finished, she said a quiet prayer. The other two were waiting in the truck when she was done.

Dane drove up to the Marshall's house, where they left the body of the Boss. The ground was slightly easier to dig in, primarily since there were deciduous trees in the area. They were able to get this one done in about twenty minutes. Before Perra walked away with a good pair of hiking shoes, she made a small cross and said another prayer.

They had a harder time with the next two bodies. The ground here was much harder to dig in, and the hole needed to fit both of them. They took turns with a shovel until they were tired. Perra soon had blisters on her palms, so she mostly just watched.

The farthest two were several minutes away and had been out in the full sun. Something had been chewing on the fleshiest parts of their faces. They were truly gruesome, and this time Perra emptied the remains of her breakfast on the ground. One had on cowboy boots, which refused to come off. The body was just too swelled up for them to come off. She did not bother with the tennis shoes the other wore.

The dirt was surprisingly softer in the area, but the hole had to be just as big as the last one. Dane and Connie took deep drafts of the still cool water as they took a break. After a short while, they continued on with their task. They would not stop until they finished.

After patting the last of the dirt on the two graves, Wayne rested with one of his hands on the top of the shovel. He breathed deeply to catch his breath, and watched his wife with a warmth the sun could not provide.

Perra, once again, had something made up as a head stone, if only a few branches tied together with some string she had brought along. Dane and Connie did not say anything as she finished her ritual. They knew she was still deeply religious, despite what had happened to the world. She blamed the devil for everything that befell on the world.

Despite their deep love, Wayne and Perra had agreed to disagree about religion. Wayne felt it was created by man to control man, even though many men throughout history had the best intentions. To him, it was inherent that man was spiritual and looked up in awe and felt that something bigger than them was present. It was something so vast and incomprehensible that they ended up worshiping the Sun, the Moon, and many other larger or lesser deities. He had seen and understood the history of man and his deceptive ways, of creating gods and hiding the truth. What it all boiled down to was greed, a need for more power and money, a need to control all.

Perra was simplistic in her approach to religion. She was born and raised in a Catholic country. There was no question in her mind, and that was that.

Wayne hated the fact that she was so closed minded, and hated even more the fact that most kids were programmed to believe something, no matter the scientific evidence that proved contrary to it. Despite that, their love was deep, and *that* was ultimately all that mattered.

Once Perra was done, they drove home in silence. They were all hopeful that Chris and Wayne were doing better, but that was not to be the case.

Frank was waiting for them at the entrance. As they pulled up, he walked out with concern written all over him. Connie could immediately tell by the way he held himself.

"He's gotten worse, hasn't he?" She had almost leapt from the truck when they stopped.

"I'm afraid so. I think we need to get to a hospital as soon as possible. There's got to be something left behind to help him." The deep, craggy lines seemed even deeper with his concern.

"Let's do it, then," Dane said, "and the sooner, the better. Let's get this stuff put up, and head into Pueblo. We still have plenty of time before it gets dark."

With a renewed sense of urgency, they went inside and cleaned up. The promised meal was there waiting for them, so they quickly ate and got ready to go.

Frank refused to stay behind, so it was he, Dane and Connie that loaded up in the truck. They each had a weapon, a canteen with fresh water and some food. Dane also grabbed a few wind-up flashlights and one of the radios. He did not think it would work from very far, but it was better than nothing if they got pinned down somewhere.

With quick goodbyes, they loaded into the truck and sped off towards the interstate. Perra watched them from the doorway as they disappeared into the distance. A lone tear slid down her cheek as she hoped they would find what they needed to help her soul mate. She wiped the tear, said a short prayer and turned around and went back inside.

CHAPTER 30
TWO BIRDS WITH ONE STONE

The truck was nearly full after they put in one of the containers of home-made gasoline. They still had one left, but did not think they would need it since they only had a round trip of less than one hundred miles.

They all sat in their own world as they sped down the highway. Some spots were slightly blown over with dirt and debris, but more than a few times they slowed down due to road damage. Weeds had sprouted in the tiniest cracks and opened them up further.

The trip was fairly uneventful, except for the roughness of the road. Still, it was in fair condition after the neglect and abuse from Mother Nature.

They saw no moving vehicles as they drove into the s-curves of the interstate. The bridges that spanned the road were still there, and thankfully not blocking their way.

Dane coasted onto the off ramp and took a left. He nearly stopped at the stop sign. Even after all this time, old habits remained. The old town seemed spooky, seeing it in such miserable shape, and empty. Many of the houses had no roofs or were utterly flattened. A few large toppled trees made him have to back track and find another way.

The hospital, only a few blocks from the highway, fared better. The windows were mostly intact, as was the roof. Many of the vehicles scattered around it were either destroyed or damaged. It looked as if a small militia had come fighting its way through here.

They were all nervous as they stopped the truck. Dane remembered where the emergency entrance was and parked as close to it as he could. He pulled out the dosimeter and did a quick reading of the area. He relaxed a little bit as he heard just a few clicks come from it.

They had their weapons up and ready as they headed to the doors. They had been powered in the past, so Dane pushed hard on one. When he put his shoulder into it, it started to open slowly. Frank walked up to the other one, turned around and with a mule kick, shattered it into thousands of pieces. He hardly reacted as he walked by Dane and into the hospital. Connie and Dane quickly glanced at each other, and then followed him inside.

The emergency room doors used to open by a button from the nurses station. Now that there was no power, the doors opened easily. They had to shoulder their weapons to crank up the flashlights, since there was very little light. They went from room to room trying to find a storage area for medicines. As they continued on, a few of the doors hung on hinges, or lay one the floor. One such room showed glass and metal shelving that lay smashed. It was the room they had been looking for. Their hearts nearly sank as their lights reflected off a glistening array of devastation. Upon closer inspection, it was just vandalism, and not deliberate destruction of the medicine.

"Shine your flashlights on the floor," Dane said. Strewn all over the floor were many small bottles of different kinds, all mixed together. After a quick search, they found what they came for.

"Yes," Connie exclaimed. "I was so afraid there wouldn't be anything left. I wonder if they were looking for psychotropic drugs." She squatted down on her haunches, then wound up her flashlight. She picked up a bottle and shined it on a label, and then another. A further search resulted in finding a box of syringes.

As they exited the building and entered the truck, a sudden thought ran through Connie's mind. "This took less than an hour to get here and find this stuff, I think we should go look around a little bit before we head back."

Frank had a perplexed look on his face as he looked at his daughter. "OK, but what about Chris? I thought you were in a hurry to get some medicine back to him."

"I am, but we only have a limited amount of fuel for this truck. A few hours more won't kill him."

"What do you have in mind," Dane asked.

"For starters, there are several junk yards about ten miles from here. We might be able to find another radiator for the truck. I also want to visit one of the large department stores."

"Those stores have got to be empty by now. Even if all of the people are gone, the roofs have probably collapsed, and the surviving animals have probably made a nice home out of the rest of it," said her father.

"Nevertheless, I need to check for myself."

"What is so pressing that you have to make your son suffer more than he needs to?" Her father pressed.

"I need some pads, okay? You have no idea how uncomfortable it is to have to use a sock or a rag for my period. Trying to clean them is next to impossible."

"Oh...sorry pumpkin." After that the guys shut up and did not say anything for a while.

Dane sympathized with her, and hid his attempt at keeping a straight face.

They passed many homes and buildings that were either burned out or had the roofs torn off. There were a few areas that had been burned to the ground, then washed away during the storms. Since then, life had returned to reclaim the property.

They kept a careful lookout as they drove up to the turn off. The paved road was washed away, but the little truck was small enough that they drove off to the side and down the dry wash. A little extra gas to get up the slight embankment and they were on the paved road again.

Many of the salvage yards were so over grown that hardly anything could be seen in them. Most of the signs had blown down, but the painted signs on the walls could still be read.

They pulled up to a faded Ford sign. Dane grabbed a small dented up tool box from behind the seat. He stepped away from the truck and slung his weapon over his shoulder, then walked over the downed fence. The area was hardly recognizable from just a few years ago.

They went from prospect to prospect but were disappointed each time. None of the few trucks that used the same radiator had one in it. On their way out they did a quick check inside the concrete block building.

Connie had her flashlight out and went down one dusty aisle. "I found some radiators. There are tags on them too," she said excitedly.

Frank and Dane helped pull one from the shelf as Connie's mood rose considerably at finding a replacement.

"Let's get another one for back-up, just in case."

"Good idea, aren't you glad I thought of that?" Her father joked.

Connie just grinned and helped with another radiator.

"It's good to know that we still have parts for the truck. From the parts on these shelves, we should be able to keep her running for years to come," Dane said. He shined his flashlight down the dusty isle. They also located a fuel pump, water pump, carburetor and alternator, which they took.

Once they loaded their bounty into the back of the truck, they headed off in another direction, toward a large department store. As they topped the ridge near the old University, they could see that the bridge ahead was washed out. Dane cussed quietly, then turned around and back tracked to the Interstate, often passing abandoned vehicles. A few minutes later he turned off the road and headed for the closest store.

The parking lot had been a scene from a horror story the likes only Steven King could write about. It was evident that people had reverted to savagery after things fell apart. They walked through the remains of cars, trucks and people.

Connie kept her eyes pointed at the darkened entryway as they made their way through the carnage. Large and small bones lay scattered together on the debris and weed-encrusted pavement.

Dane and Frank held their weapons ready, with their flashlights pointing where ever the barrel went. Connie kept her weapon shouldered as she used her flashlight to lead the way. Skeletons lay scattered here too.

They stepped over more rubble, debris and bones here than

they did outside. No food in any container could be seen. The only things left were books, magazines, clothing, cleaning supplies, personal hygiene and frivolous junk that high pitched voices used to beg for.

Small carrying baskets that shoppers used were lying all over. Connie filled several with hygiene items for men and women. Most of those shelves were hardly touched.

"What a relief," Connie said as she stuffed another basket full of pads. "Let's get the hell out of here."

They waded through the store, then through the parking lot in silence. They did not bother to unload the baskets and quickly set them in the back. A few minutes later they were back on the Interstate and heading south.

The drive back went uneventfully. They hardly talked about the visions of dead men, women and children. Many of them still had hair attached, as well as faded and torn clothing. The skeletal grins would no doubt trouble them in their dreams for a while.

Dane did not bother to use any of the alternate routes through the trees. He drove as straight up to the shelter as he could.

When Connie pounded on the inner door with her rifle butt, June and Perra came out to help them with the supplies.

Dane, with Connie's help, immediately went to Chris and prepared a spot on his shoulder for a shot. Connie cleaned the area as best she could as Dane drew the precious fluid into the syringe. They were not sure how much to give him, so he filled it up about half way, made sure no air was in the needle, then plunged it into his shoulder. They quickly repeated the procedure on Wayne.

The women fairly fawned over the feminine packages when they saw them. They went inside with the goodies, and Perra went through it all and started storing the pads, razors, shaving cream, deodorant, toothpaste, toothbrushes, combs, brushes, and various bars of resplendent smelling soap.

Wayne had stocked up on all of those items, but he had only planned on four, maybe five people living in the shelter. Now that they had eight people, his supplies would quickly shrink.

Within a few days, Chris' fever had gone down and felt much better. Wayne only had a mild fever, but that too improved. Everyone's mood started to get back to normal as their health improved. After they were back on their feet, albeit cautiously, they decided to have a celebration dinner.

By the time the food was ready and the table loaded, they were all washed, shaved and dressed in their nicest clothing.

Frank surprised them all with some home-brewed alcohol. Evidently he had found the time and resources to build a still. He had kept disappearing for a while each day, with hardly a word. They questioned him about it, but he said he needed some breathing room.

For the first time in what seemed like ages, they laughed and joked. A few of them got drunk. They all felt fine and were ready to go on with their lives, until June requested that they return the truck to the compound.

"I think we should take it back, so they can at least get around," she explained to Wayne. We'll still have Connie's truck to get around in."

"What makes you think they don't have any other vehicles?"

"When we were going out the front entrance, I glanced

back at the Boss' motor home. Not only was it on fire, but so were both of the carports. It looked like all of the trucks were on fire, as well. Now that the Boss is dead and out of the way, I truly believe they will form a democracy, instead of the theocracy that kept the women virtual sex slaves. I know that most of the motor homes still run, but you can't take them over rough roads. They will need the truck."

Dane and Frank, who overheard the conversation, were arm and arm and slightly weaving as they came over and sat down.

"They can't have the fuckin' truck. It's our prize, an' we need it," Frank managed.

June turned to Frank with fire in her eyes. "What do you know you drunk old fool? Many of those people are my friends, and a few were just young girls at the Junior High School I worked at." Flames grew hot in her cheeks. "You don't know what we have all been through with that "villain", she nearly spat the word. Even *I* wasn't safe from his groping hands and horrible breath. Some of those girls had hardly even started their periods before he "Planted the seeds of Mother Earth" in them. It makes me want to puke!"

Frank sat back in his drunken stupor. He seemed to have a hard time focusing on June as he tried to think. "Oh, well... it's *our* truck," he slurred.

Connie heard the heated exchange between her father and the normally placid woman and came over. "Come on Dad, I think you need some fresh air." She got a shoulder under his and helped him down the stairs and outside. The brisk-cold dry air barely seemed to affect him as she walked him further from the entrance.

"What's gotten up her butt?" He asked loudly.

"She's just concerned about her friends. They probably don't even know what happened to her, and right now she doesn't know what's happening to them.

Back inside, June and Wayne continued on with their conversation.

"The fact of the matter is that we don't know the situation there. We cannot take the chance that they will use the truck to come after us again, no matter how remote that possibility might be," he said playing the devil's advocate.

"I can understand your point of view," June replied evenly, "but since we don't know the current situation there, maybe we can get the Ford fixed. Then, using the protection from it, we can head over to see what the status of the compound is."

"It sounds like you've been thinking a lot about this," Wayne said.

"It's almost the only thing I *can* think of," she replied.

"Well, that's pretty much what I've been thinking too. It's been bothering me about all of those lives that were lost, and not knowing what happened to the compound has been eating at me. There are just too many young kids that could be hurt by what we did. I've come to the conclusion that now that the Boss is dead and the place is hopefully safe, that we could try and make amends. Giving them back the truck, will go a long way in establishing some trust between us."

"Trust me, now that the Boss and a several of his devout followers are dead, they will probably kiss your butt. The women were not happy, and several of the men were not happy with the situation either. Almost all of the people that didn't want to give up their wives or daughters usually disappeared."

"I didn't know it was that bad," Wayne said with a sad shake of his head.

"It was far worse, but I don't want to talk about it. About the only good that came out of our little community was that we were well organized. We produced a lot of food, considering the growing season up here."

"OK, but let's also consider that the Boss' friends are still there and in charge. They will be better prepared this time and won't be pulling any punches."

"You know, I've been a teacher and a librarian for most of my life. I've always relied upon facts to make decisions. But right now, from what I saw as we left the compound, I just have a strong feeling that everything is fine." She sat at the table with her eyes focused on the event from just a few weeks prior. The still image was crystal clear in her minds' eye as she focused on the kids she had cared for.

"Let's hope so, but if we are going to go, we need to do it before very much snow is on the ground. The roads are bad enough when we can see them. With snow drifts hiding most of the ground, it will be too dangerous to be caught out in it."

The party soon wound down, and everyone bedded down for the night.

The next day brought a light dusting of snow, with a promise of more. No sooner had they started to prepare to leave, when heavy clouds drifted in to linger and drop their load. Somewhat impatiently, they waited for the late autumn snowfall to melt. The temperature during the day nibbled at forty degrees while the night plunged into the twenties. The wind picked up considerably and was relentless as it sped through the trees, causing snow drifts to pile up as high as four feet. They waited another day, and then another. After a few more days, Frank started to get impatient. "What are we waiting for? We could have been there and back by now." He had been pacing lately and was doing so now.

"Are you kidding?" June asked. "Have you ever had frostbite? That wind out there has the wind chill down to a dangerous level. A person, especially an old one, wouldn't last more than an hour in it."

"I'm not talking about being *in* it. I'm talking about being in a *truck*, in it. The heater works fine, and we have lots of shovels if we get struck. I'm just tired of not doing anything. Since everyone else is determined to get rid of our back up truck, we might as well get to it. And yes, I've *had* frostbite. I almost lost a few toes to it."

June and Frank, after their initial attraction, never seemed to get along very well, especially when it came to the truck. Most of the time they spent their time apart, just so they would not argue, but the shelter was just not large enough to do that for very long.

One day after lunch, Wayne could sense a change in Perra. He could tell for the last few days that something was eating at her more and more. Privacy was hardly anything they had now, so he had to pull her into the bathroom, shut the door, and ask her what was bothering her.

"I've been thinking about my family again," she said with her head down.

Although Wayne still had their original plan in the back of his head, he had not thought much of it after they got tangled up with the Boss. He still wanted to try and find a ham radio, but the opportunity to find one during the coming winter was dwindling. "I'm sorry we weren't able to find a way to contact your family, sweetheart, but it looks like we might be snowed in for a while."

She looked up with watery eyes, "I know, but I just miss them. Now that things have been quiet lately, my thoughts have turned to them again. It's been over two years since I've talked to my family. I don't even know if they are still alive..." she managed.

Wayne quietly held her tight. Her body shook with quiet sobs. Everything that had befallen on them had been hardest on her. He felt that, even though she seemed the most sensitive of their group, she was also one of the strongest. He did not know how he would feel if he had moved to a different country, a different culture, and lost contact with his family. The Filipinos that he had seen and known only for a short while, during his trips to the Philippines, had been remarkably close to their family and roots. Multiple generations often lived in the same home, as had her family. They had their trials and tribulations but were decent people.

After a few more days of waiting for the snow to melt off enough to drive safely, Wayne gathered a few people together to make the trip. Even though the nights had been down in the teens and twenties, the 10 AM morning sun had warmed the air up to a tolerable thirty-eight degrees. More importantly, the sun was shining on the ground.

"I'm tired of sitting around," complained his older brother, who had been arguing about going on the trip.

"I know, Dane, but your arm hasn't fully healed. It's just not worth the risk of injuring it more just to get you out of here for a while."

"What about your leg? You want to go when it isn't fully healed?"

"I can drive a stick shift with my right leg hurt. Can you drive one with your right arm hurt?"

"Probably not," he conceded. He had been scratching at the ace bandage lately, and could not seem to get to the itch properly. His left leg was mostly healed by now.

When Wayne had approached Connie about going a look of disgust, and something else he could not read, quickly crossed her face. He knew she might have a hard time returning to the place where she was kidnaped. But she was one of the few that was healthy, and able to handle a weapon well. She knew it too, and her look turned to one of acceptance. She merely looked Wayne in the eyes, tightened her grip on her hunting rifle, and nodded. Wayne beamed her a smile, for he was glad that she could rebound from the thought of what had lain in wait for her, had they not rescued her.

Since the truck was too small to fit three people in the cab comfortably, especially on the bumpy roads, Frank volunteered to sit in back. After bundling up with multiple layers of clothing, he grabbed a few blankets.

"This ought to keep me warm," he said as he waddled out to the truck. A few of them suppressed their giggles as he struggled to climb into the back.

Susan still was not up to traveling, and June and Perra had no inclination to go. They were needed more at home than on a trip to return the truck. Everyone came out to see them off, to wish them luck, and to hurry home.

Wayne and Connie went through a list of everything they thought they would need, and checked it off as it went into the back of the truck.

"That looks like everything," Connie said as she checked off the last item.

"Not quite everything," Wayne said as he turned to his wife.

Connie rechecked her list and was perplexed for a few seconds. After turning to reply to Wayne, she saw him give his wife a long hug. She immediately went to Chris and gave him a hug, and then Susan and the other women.

"Be safe, honey ko," Perra pleaded, "come back soon, huh?

"Don't worry, sweetheart, we should be back in four or five hours. If we have any trouble, we'll head straight back, okay?

"Ok, but you know I will worry about you."

"I know, but we have to know what happened to the people in the compound. Once we know that there is no threat and the others are okay, we'll all breathe easier."

June surprised everyone by stepping up to the back of the truck, "be careful, you old fool," she said with a slight smile and a glimmer in her eyes. Frank nodded mutely in surprise.

Perra waved to her husband and stepped back as they got in the truck. It had been running for several minutes and was nice and warm inside. With a quick wave, they headed down to the road.

Wayne wished he could turn on the radio and listen to some music. He carefully drove down the slightly mushy road. Music certainly would help with his nerves. Every time he thought about the Boss and his followers, his heart sped up. The man had been just too unpredictable, and that made him extremely dangerous. He went over the different scenarios as if the Boss' allies were alive, and if they were dead. Either way, his main priority was to get the other truck and *then* see what they were up against. With snow everywhere it was a greater risk, for if...*Damn*, he thought, *there are just too many "Ifs". How the hell am I supposed to plan...calm down...calm down*, he thought. *Just take a breath and re-center yourself.* After a few deep breaths, he calmed down and just focused on driving. *It is what it is*, he thought as he continued to find his center. After about twenty-five minutes of driving Wayne pulled up to the old Ford. He could hear Connie sigh a huge sigh of relief when they saw the truck was still in the same condition that they left it.

There were small drifts of snow around the truck and across the road, but there were no tracks leading up to the truck. They quickly unloaded the radiator and tools and got to work. Wayne grabbed a plastic pail and put it under the lower radiator hose as Connie undid the connections. Frank got out the tool kit, which had been in the front of the truck, and made short work of the bolts holding it in place. After several minutes, they had it out and were replacing it with the other one. Several minutes later Wayne was pouring the remaining precious liquid back into the new radiator, then he topped it off with water.

Connie anxiously unlocked the truck and slid inside. After holding her breath for a few seconds, she turned the key. After the engine had turned over a few times, it leapt to life. She nearly cried as she silently thanked her husband for taking such good care of it for her. They cleaned up and loaded the tools and pail into the back of the Ford. They tossed the old radiator off to the side of the road.

Frank went to the back of the truck and pulled off the dead branches that still clung to the back of the bumper.

Connie jumped back in the truck, while her father got in the back. She carefully turned the truck around and headed down the treacherous road. A few spots had small trickles of water crossing their path, but with hardly slowing down, they made it back to the paved road. The snow on the black top had mostly melted off. There were many spots where the trees shadowed the roadway, but the unrelenting sun made short work of it once the shadow moved. They had talked about different times to make their appearance if the way was clear. A later arrival time, they hoped, would give the sun time to do its work.

They did not know if there would be trees barring their way, a ditch perhaps, or even rocks. They could not predict what was ahead of them, so they went in slowly. After a few miles, the only thing they encountered was some icy areas that the sun had not reached yet. When they came within sight of the compound, they found it pretty much the same as before, but this time they saw no movement within. After several minutes of waiting, Connie briefly honked the horn.

"I don't see anything," called Frank.

Connie waved Wayne up beside her. "We haven't seen anything, not even smoke from a chimney. What do you think? Do you think they are hiding?

Wayne could not believe that they would hide from them. They came in peace the first time and the second time they only came for one of their people. He studied the two well-burned areas of the wall. He could clearly see the damage to what remained of the motor home. Raising up his binoculars, he could see that there was nobody about, but what caught his eye was that several of the motor homes were missing.

"It looks like they moved out," he said after a minute.

"I don't think they liked living in those cold motor homes and trailers. I'll bet you a pound of flap-jacks that they moved back into the houses down the road. That probably means that they aren't under somebody's thumb," Frank said as he looked out the small window.

"Let's go check it out," Connie suggested.

"You lead, I'll follow," replied Wayne.

Connie started up the truck and slowly drove down the road, then turned to the right and drove straight up to the opening of the compound. The dirt in the trench had been filled in and, by the looks of it, had been driven over many times. To the left of the opening were two graves. Connie continued into the enclosure and made a slow circuit before coming back out to where Wayne was waiting. She pulled up beside him, "the place is deserted. It doesn't look like they've been here for a few weeks. All of the tracks are faded, and the snow in the shadows don't have *any* tracks."

"So they left soon after we did. That's some good news for a change. Let's take a look at those graves. Maybe there will be some names on them.

Connie pulled the truck over so it would protect them from the opening of the compound, just in case someone was still hiding inside. Frank stayed inside with his weapon ready.

Wayne walked with Connie from grave to grave. They only recognized Jose's name. The other marker showed a mans name too, but they did not recognize it.

"Well, it could have been worse," he said as he stepped back into the truck.

"Maybe we can find something inside."

This time Wayne followed Connie inside the deserted compound. They pulled up to the shack that used to house many of the women and children, and then waited there for a few minutes. There was nobody to be seen, so Wayne got out of the truck and quickly went into the building. He smoothly un-shouldered his weapon. He did not want to stay outside very long, but did not want to rush inside either, he risked exposing himself either way. The simple latch on the door seemed loud as it banged shut. Stepping in he did a quick scan. All of the chairs and tables were gone, as well as the curtains that had adorned the long row of windows. With his weapon up he headed to the large kitchen at the end of the building. He stopped outside the large doorway and peeked inside. It was just as he suspected. None of the cooking supplies remained, so he nosed through the simple cupboards. They, too, were empty. *Whew*, he thought. *Unless someone was desperate for a place to live, they sure would not remain here.* He figured they moved back to town. Winter months could be bitter cold in the Rocky Mountains, so they probably headed back to the thicker, more insulated homes they had left behind. He turned and walked back out of the kitchen and out the exit. Instead of trying to take cover, he just walked to the next building, which use to have a few motor homes between it and the kitchen. That was empty, as well as the next few. By the time he made it to the Boss' wrecked motor home, it was obvious that nobody remained in the compound.

As Wayne stood surveying the carnage they had wrought, a slight breezed wafted over the wreckage. The smell of burnt wood, plastic and gasoline wafted his way. Despite the odor, Wayne felt his spirits lift just a little more.

"The place is empty. Let's go check San Isabel," he said. He looked around one more time, then climbed back into the truck.

Connie started up her truck and headed back out toward the pavement. Frank sat back down for a short rest since his side hurt from holding the rifle up to his shoulder. Wayne started up the smaller truck and followed them.

The small town of San Isabel had been around for many decades. A few of the houses were over one hundred years old, and looked as if they would be around for a while longer. Although work there had been sparse, most of the people were either retired, or commuted to work. Like most isolated towns, there was an eclectic assortment of houses. They ranged from the very old, to very modern.

As they approached the small town, Connie slowed down to a crawl, and then stopped. She could see smoke from many of the houses in the area. A lazy haze of light blue smoke drifted serenely out of town and down the valley.

Frank stood in the back with the binoculars working overtime.

"There are a few people just outside of the restaurant," he said.

"They don't appear to be armed."

"Can you see anyone else outside?" She asked.

"No... not from this angle. There might be more, but we'll have to pull up...oh, they've seen us."

The two people that were standing near the restaurant had been taking a break from splitting wood. The woman had been setting up wood on a block, and the man had been splitting it. After taking a few minutes for a breather, they changed places and started to continue. When the man bent down to get a short log, the woman spotted the truck. She recognized it immediately and pointed to it as she told her companion. He stood up and stared but did nothing hostile.

Connie stayed there as the others continued to stare at the truck. She thought she recognized the woman from the compound, but not the man. After a few tense moments, they started walking toward the truck. She could plainly see that they were not armed. The woman suddenly raised her right arm and waved. She also seemed to be smiling at them.

"Keep an eye out for me," she said as she opened the door and stepped out behind it.

"Connie...no, don't go...damn it," Frank cursed quietly.

"Are you the people that came to the compound before?" The woman asked from several yards away.

"Yes. Aren't you the one that brought me some food?" The woman had a quizzical look on her face. Connie clarified, "I was locked up in a small trailer a few weeks ago when my friends came back for me."

The curly haired woman looked at the man beside her, then back to Connie, who was now out in plain sight. "Yes, I took some food there, but I did not get a good look at who was in the trailer. They told me not to talk to you." Then she beamed a huge smile, "But now I can, everyone can! We haven't seen or heard from the Boss. We saw him and the others take off after you. What happened? Where are the rest of your friends? Are they here?

Connie pondered her questions carefully. "The boss is dead."

She decided to change the subject. "So everyone is OK now?" She asked.

The young woman laughed a little, "Oh yes, everyone is just fine now that we know the Boss is dead!"

"We didn't know what happened and had to risk coming back to see if you were OK. Since you are, we want to give you back your truck."

The couple came within a few feet of the truck and stopped. They looked a little nervous when they saw Frank in the small window with a rifle barrel sticking out.

The man called up to the window, "It's OK. You won't need that here."

The woman had that quizzical look again.

"Our truck? Oh yeah. Where are the guys that took off after you?" She looked slightly uncomfortable. "What happened to the rest of them?"

"I'm sorry, but they didn't make it," Connie replied carefully.

The woman's face had a look of grief. "Really? What happened?"

Connie gave them the short version of the tragedy.

"I'm sorry to hear that, especially about Tony. He was a good kid. He just got caught up with some of the others." She brightened a little.

"But the others, good riddance! Were any of you hurt?"

"Half of us got hurt, one way or another," replied Connie sullenly, "but everyone will be OK."

"We are glad to hear it," she said as her partner shook his head in agreement.

"Most of us were very unhappy and had been planning a coup when you showed up. We didn't know if it would work or not, but you ended up solving our problem for us. For that, we are eternally grateful. We were hoping you would come back, so we could offer you a place to live. We've lost too many good people, and we'd be honored if you'd join us."

By this time, Wayne had driven up to them. He finished rolling down the window as he stopped. He caught the last part of the conversation and was extremely relieved. He got out and Connie introduced him, then herself and her father, who had come out of the back of the truck.

"I'm Melissa, and this is Larry. You can call me Missy."

A few minutes later, others recognized the trucks and came down to meet them. Word of the Boss' death spread quickly. They came in anticipation of meeting the people that had freed them from oppression and abuse. A few went back to their homes and returned with gifts of food and other supplies. Soon afterward, someone brought down the weapons that they had been forced to leave. Connie was ecstatic at getting her favorite hunting rifle back.

"Are you gonna stay? A little girl with big blue eyes asked as she stood by her mother.

Connie bent down to her eye level, "I'm sorry hon, but my family is expecting us back soon."

The little girl pondered for a second, then said, "They can come here too. There are lots and lots of houses to live in," she said as she spread her arms wide.

"Maybe another time sweetheart, but right now we have hurt people that have to rest up before they can go anywhere." Connie reached out and held one rosy cheek, "But thanks for inviting us," she said with a smile.

The little girl beamed a smile and said, "You're welcome."

After an hour of chatting with the people of the town, they announced that they had to get back to the others, before they started to worry.

"We'll probably be back in the spring, but can't promise anything right now," Wayne said after he shook hands with a few dozen people."

"Bye," rang out a crystal-clear little girl's voice. "Come back soon."

All three of them loaded into the front of the truck, then headed back up the road. They were deep in thought as they headed back home. They were astonished at the reception they had received after everyone found out they were there. There had only been a few hostile glares from the crowd, and they figured they must have been friends or relatives of the party that tried to kill them. All in all, they felt good for helping to get them out of a bad situation. One which happened all too many times throughout history.

CHAPTER 31
ANOTHER WINTER

Upon returning home with the good news, they had another party. This time almost everybody got drunk, including the normally reserved June. Now that she knew her friends were safe, she let loose, and ended up being the first one to pass out. They feasted on the gifts from their new friends, as well as from the storage at the Marshall's place. For the first time in what seemed like ages, they were truly content. Most of them drifted off to much nicer dreams than they had in a long while. Frank started sleeping in the fake bunker. They found and brought in a narrow bed for June. They placed it against the wall, under the left set of steps. Chris and Susan took the center bed.

Winter announced its presence with a vengeance a few days later, as snow fell in their little area of the world, surrounding them in a quiet layer of white. Occasionally they ventured outside for a little fun, and once in a while they made a trip to get a few more supplies at the Marshall's. Except for Frank and June, each of the couple took turns making the trip, since that was the only privacy they had, and while they were there, they took full advantage of it.

As December turned to January, they celebrated the new year with more of Franks strong alcohol. They went through the games and played them until they got bored with them again, and most of them read many of the books they stored for just such an occasion. January crept slowly out of sight as a snowy February came on strong.

One clear, cool morning in mid March, Wayne got up early, grabbed his rifle, bow and arrows, a few other supplies and headed out of the shelter. The snow was mostly gone, and the buds on the trees and bushes were pronounced. He stood by a certain tree as the sun came up, patiently watching the narrow trail that led to his snare. The heavily snow capped mountains in the distance were seen through crystal clear air. Waiting for a rabbit to come along, he reflected on the peace and contentment he felt in his surroundings. He marveled at the ebb and flow of life, and of his and his family's place in it. Within a few weeks of each other, Connie and Susan announced that they were pregnant. That too, led to another party, with the two women abstaining from the powerful alcohol. Wayne's thoughts soon turned to the issue of space. By the end of fall, there would be two more mouths to feed, and crying babies in the middle of the night would wreak havoc on them all. They would soon be leaving their home for Connie's spacious rancher. Chris and Susan had even talked of taking over the Marshall's place, since the rancher only had so many bedrooms. Besides that, they just wanted more time alone together.

Wayne took in the sights and breathed in the clean, fresh air. He thought about their quest to find a ham radio, and the feeling of failure at letting his wife down. At some point, he knew, they would find one and finally answer her burning questions. For now, he felt at peace At the same time wondered about the future. *What will man-kind amount to?* He asked himself. *Will we ever stop abusing and taking advantage of each other? Can we learn to live with mother nature and* all *of her creatures, without spoiling it for our children? Will we* ever *grow up?*

He pondered many thoughts, until a slight movement caught his attention. Moving just his eyes, he saw a fat rabbit walk into his snare. The loop closed tightly around its neck as the scared rabbit tried to run. Wayne quickly walked over to the rabbit and with a quick movement, pulled the loop off of its neck. He straightened up as the rabbit ran off, wishing it a long life.

"Today is a new beginning!" He said to the terrified rabbit. He packed his snare away and walked back to his spot by the tree. Shades of pink colored the sky as he took it all in, reveling in the circle of life, in the early morning Colorado twilight.

The Beginning